FAIRFORD AFFAIRS

BOOK 2

UNRAVELLING Well

BAY SINCLAIR

Unravelling Nell

Copyright © 2023 by Bay Sinclair

All rights reserved.

Cover designed by Florida Girl Design Inc. (www.gobookcoverdesign.com)

The characters and events portrayed in this book are fictitious or are used fictitiously. Any similarity to real persons, living or dead, is purely coincidental and not intended by the author. The author does not endorse any behavior carried out by any character in this work of fiction or any other.

This story includes elements that may not be suitable for some readers. Though they don't appear on the page, there are mentions of past self-harm and abuse. Readers who may be sensitive to these elements, please take note.

To Barbara, for helping me learn my self-worth and find my strength.

And to Jason, always and forever.

Also by Bay Sinclair

Fairford Affairs
Fixing Olivia

CHAPTER 1

Nell

Nell slid a snifter of brandy and a glass of the house white across the bar to Master Donovan. He and his longtime sub, Meredith, spent every Saturday night at Valhalla like clockwork and were two of her favorite customers. She loved watching them interact, seeing the mutual respect and adoration in their dynamic. None of her past relationships ever came close to that.

"Thanks," Master Donovan said, sliding a fifty-dollar bill across the bar. "Keep the change."

That was reason number two for their favorite status—the smallest denomination Master Donovan ever carried was a fifty, and he seemed to find change cumbersome.

Grabbing the drinks, he set off through the center of the club's main floor, weaving between people and dungeon furniture toward the tables by the stage. She could just make out Meredith in the dim lighting, awaiting her Master's return to their booth. They always scheduled their play around the midnight show.

Nell checked her watch. It read twenty minutes to midnight; she knew from experience she was about to be incredibly busy. Valhalla had a two-drink limit, and the most popular times to indulge were upon arrival and during the performance. The owners and bouncers found it hard to keep things safe, sane, and consensual when patrons got plastered.

Sure enough, the closer they got to showtime, the more the main floor emptied. Some people even trickled out of the back hallway, which held the club's five private rooms. And everyone wanted a drink before they sat down.

She was in the zone tonight, flying through drink orders with a grace and speed that kept those tips right on coming. If things kept up like this, it would only be another couple of weeks before she could replace her laptop. That was close to the bottom of her list—a want-to-have, not a need-to-have. But she'd worked her way through the rest of the list faster than she ever thought she could, moving out of that shitty motel into an actual apartment, getting a used smartphone with a brand-new number, and restoring most of her wardrobe. She could afford to be a little frivolous.

The stage lights turned on at the exact moment the music changed to a softer, slower beat, revealing two figures at centerstage. Jasper and Penny were another regular D/s pair at the club, who both had a serious exhibitionism kink. They did shows once a month, as much for their own pleasure as for the audience's.

The crimson and violet lights painted Penny's pale skin and short, white-blond hair, making her look even more like a pixie than usual. Jasper's hand circled her throat, his dark skin a perfect contrast to hers, his chiseled muscles a counterpoint to her slight frame.

Jesus Christ, they looked beautiful together. It struck Nell anew every single time she saw them, as if she somehow convinced herself she remembered wrong over and over again. And yet, another night at the club would roll around, and it would practically hurt to watch them again. Like looking at the sun.

"Why are we here tonight, Penny?" Jasper asked, his deep voice carrying all the way to Nell's end of the dungeon.

"Because I need to be punished, Sir."

Jasper's other hand came up to rest possessively on her breast. "And you need these people to witness your punishment, don't you? It's the only way you'll feel like you've atoned for your sins."

Nell felt those words reverberate through her, like electricity dancing just beneath the surface of her skin.

Atone for your sins.

Fuck, what she wouldn't give to be the one up on that stage. Before Micah, she would've been. But now? Fear and lust tangled together inside her, keeping her hidden behind the bar, always safe and out of reach.

"Yes, Sir." Penny rested her head against his bare chest, but she never took her eyes off the audience. "Please help me."

Nell leaned forward, her forearms resting on the smooth surface of the bar. Jasper and Penny's shows were by far her favorites. It wasn't even a competition. Not only did she have the biggest crush imaginable on both of them, but Jasper's severity made him so much more captivating than the other Doms who performed. Nell's heart pounded as she waited to see what they planned for this month's scene.

"The Mistress wants to see you in her office."

Someone whispered the words in Nell's ear, and she jumped about a foot in the air. She whipped around to find Amber, one of the dungeon monitors.

"Jesus," Nell said, putting a hand over her chest. "I almost had a heart attack."

"Sorry," Amber said, smirking. "I should've been more careful. I know how distracted you get when Jasper and Penny scene."

Nell laughed and gestured to the nearly empty floor. "I'm clearly not the only one."

"Touché." Amber's dark eyes danced with amusement. "You can head on back. Mistress Freya asked me to watch the bar."

Trying not to let her disappointment show, Nell thanked her friend and headed toward the back hallway. It would be a month before Jasper and Penny did another show. Did the Mistress really need to see her *right now*?

With a sigh, she headed down the hallway, past the private playrooms and locker rooms. When she reached the door all the way at the end, she rapped three times.

"Enter."

Nell pushed open the black-painted door, blinking as she stepped into the brightly lit office. "You wanted to see me, Mistress?"

Mistress Freya was a tall, broad woman in her late fifties, with the most piercing blue eyes Nell had ever seen. Her auburn hair fell in a riot of curls down past her shoulder blades, streaked liberally with white. Dressed in her usual black leather, she looked every bit as powerful and commanding as her goddess namesake implied.

Each time Nell walked into her office, she had to resist the urge to drop to her knees and beg for forgiveness, even if she couldn't remember doing anything wrong.

"Take a seat, kitten."

Nell settled into one of the two leather armchairs facing her boss's desk, curling her legs up under her. Her tendency to sit in that position had earned her the nickname not long after she started. "Is everything all right, Mistress?" She tried to sound casual, but some of her trepidation clearly bled through.

Mistress Freya gave her a soothing smile. "Relax. You're not in trouble."

Then why did she have to miss the show? It sure felt like a punishment.

Knowing full well that voicing the thought would be a very bad idea, she pressed her lips together and waited.

"I know you're frustrated I called you in here during Jasper and Penny's performance." She looked down her hooked nose as she said it, giving her such an intense *don't-try-to-lie-to-me-little-girl* Domme look that Nell squirmed. "Aren't you?"

"I'm sorry, Mistress," she said automatically.

But Mistress Freya shook her head. "You have nothing to be sorry for. I already told you you're not in trouble."

Nell bit her bottom lip as she tried to work out what was going on. In the end, she had no choice but to admit, "I'm confused."

"I'm going to be extremely frank with you. And I'm going to ask you to listen to everything I say, then count to ten before you respond. Can you do that for me?"

"Of course." After the way Mistress Freya took her in, she'd do just about anything the older woman asked. Freya not only gave her the job

4

at the club, but she even rented Nell the in-law apartment over her garage, getting her out of a disgusting pay-by-the-week motel.

"Good girl." Mistress Freya smiled warmly, and it washed over Nell like sunlight heating her skin. "I see the way you watch Jasper and Penny, and anyone else who plays rough on the main floor. I see the desire in your eyes and the way your breath quickens. It's obvious how much you crave it. And yet you're not doing anything about it."

Nell's brows drew together. "That's cause I'm working. I can't just—"

"Remember what I asked of you," Mistress Freya interrupted, brows arched, voice stern but not angry.

Right. Listen to everything and wait before responding. "Sorry, Mistress."

With a small nod of acknowledgement, she continued. "You're correct that I obviously expect you to keep your pants on while on the clock." One corner of her mouth lifted in a sardonic smile. "That's a given. But you only work here Wednesday through Sunday. Numerous Doms and Dommes in this club would gladly scene with you on your off days if you asked them. In fact, as I understand it, more than a few have approached you since you started here. And yet, you do two things and two things only: work in my club and sit in your apartment alone."

Okay, so maybe renting a room from her boss wasn't quite as awesome as she thought. She wanted to point out she'd visited more than a dozen of Tampa's beaches in the last few months, and also went to the gym three times a week, thank you very much.

If Mistress Freya dug into the reasons for her newfound interest in weight training and the free women's self-defense classes at the Y, though . . . it wouldn't exactly help her case. So she bit her tongue, staring at the surface of the desk between them and trying to ignore the blush heating her cheeks.

"Look at me, please," Mistress Freya said, her voice softening.

Raising her gaze took a monumental effort. Nell's heart was beating against her ribs like the wings of a trapped bird.

"I'll be the first to admit I don't know your whole story." Those bright blue eyes were so kind. So incredibly gentle. "But I do know people don't show up in a new town with nothing but the clothes on their back for a *good* reason."

Shit, shit, shit. Nell did *not* want to get into this. Not now, not ever.

"I've had a lot of subs come through my doors since I opened Valhalla. I can recognize the signs of someone who's been hurt by a person they thought they could trust."

Nell closed her eyes against the threat of tears. How could Mistress Freya do this to her? Her boss was the first person who made her feel safe in an extremely long time, and now *this*. It felt like a fucking ambush.

The clicks of stiletto heels on hardwood reverberated through the room. Then a gentle hand cupped Nell's chin. "Please, kitten. Open your eyes for me."

Forcing out a long, jagged breath, Nell did as she was told. Mistress Freya crouched down in front of her, putting them eye to eye, their noses nearly touching.

"I'm not trying to hurt you right now. And I'm not going to force you to talk about something before you're ready. But I also see how much you've been struggling. How desperately you long for what you need. How ruthlessly you deny yourself."

Tears sprang to Nell's eyes again. The Mistress was right. Of course she was right—she always was. Ever since she got away from Micah, she hadn't been able to let down her guard enough to trust another Dom for even a single scene. What if it happened all over again? She'd already proven she couldn't trust her own judgement.

"If you keep this up, you're going to explode. And when you do, you'll find what you need by whatever means necessary. That's a dangerous state of mind to be in when doing the things we do." Mistress Freya released her chin and leaned back against the desk, folding her hands placidly in her lap. "If you'll let me, I'd like to help you."

She knew she wasn't allowed to speak, so she put all her hope into her eyes instead. If anyone could help her, Mistress Freya could.

"I know someone who can reintroduce you to the lifestyle—someone I know beyond a shadow of a doubt you can trust." Her eyes crinkled at the corners. "I give you my word, he'll only hurt you in ways you'll like. And he'll help you learn what a healthy relationship between a Dominant and submissive feels like. Perhaps that'll give you the courage you need to find someone new and try again. So, what do you say?"

With a few slow, deep breaths, Nell counted to ten. Then she let nearly a year of unfulfilled desire and desperation fill her voice when she said, "*Please.*"

CHAPTER 2

Rafe

A call interrupted the song blaring from Rafe's phone while he did bicep curls in his home gym. Putting down the thirty-pound dumbbells with a small grunt, he grabbed his phone.

Grinning, he slid the green icon to the right. "Freya, my life, my love, my dream." He used that sexy, gravelly voice all submissives loved, but which he knew did absolutely nothing for the woman on the other end of the line. "Ready to turn switch for me yet?"

Her laugh came through the line low and husky—the product of decades of smoking. It made her sound like an old Hollywood starlet. "You wish, pretty boy."

Rafe's smile only widened. He couldn't put into words what it meant to hear Freya joking around again. It had been a brutal two years after Ian, her husband and longtime sub, passed away. Ian had been the beating heart of Freya's life, and without him, she'd been utterly lost.

Only after Rafe and a few of her other past mentees banded together, all but forcing her to return to teaching, did the darkness begin to lift. Giving classes to those new to the scene, helping them unleash their inner Dom or sub, and watching them flourish in the community . . . it gave meaning to her life again. Then she opened

Valhalla, building herself a new family to love and watch over and protect.

He didn't think it was an exaggeration to say her club saved her life.

"Oh well." He heaved a dramatic sigh. "I always knew you were too good for me."

Freya snorted. The woman was technically old enough to be his mother, and didn't have a submissive bone in her body—and neither did Rafe. But that didn't mean the game wasn't fun to play.

"So," Rafe said, plopping down on the weight bench. "To what do I owe the pleasure?"

"I have a favor to ask."

"Anything." He didn't hesitate. Freya had been there for him during the hardest time of his life, helping him figure out exactly the type of Dom he wanted to be. She'd even introduced him to Jonathan and Mason, two of the founding partners of Fairford Manor, where he now worked. The BDSM resort took the term *dream job* to a whole new level, especially after the founders made him a partner.

In other words, Rafe owed everything to her.

With a hum of satisfaction, Freya said, "I knew I could count on you. Check your email."

Putting her on speaker, he maneuvered to the mail app, opening the one from Freya. There was nothing in the body of the email—only an attachment. "This better not be porn," he joked as he tapped on the attachment icon.

His eyebrows arched as soon as the document opened. It was a scanned copy of a Manor application.

"You know we only accept applications by mail," he said, though his gaze flew across the tiny words on his phone screen.

Freya gave an annoyed huff. "I mailed the original. But I don't want to wait for you to get it. I want to talk about Nell now."

Rafe repressed a chuckle. Clearly nothing had changed; this Domme only did things on her schedule. There was no point in resisting.

According to the application, Nell Beaumont was a thirty-six-year-old submissive living outside Tampa and working at Valhalla. She recently got out of an eleven-year relationship, and wanted one of the Manor Doms to help ease her back into the casual side of the lifestyle.

"If you want her to come here, you know I'll say yes." Rafe studied the photo taped to her application—long dark hair, a hint of mystery in her smile, and enough muscle in her arms and thighs that he suspected she did at least some weight training. Stunning really. The thought of a strong woman like that all soft and pliant in his arms had his cock stirring.

"Good. I'll—"

"But why me?" Rafe interrupted. "Are you telling me there isn't a single Dom in your club who'll scene with her?" And if that was the case, what the fuck was wrong with her?

"Oh, there are plenty," Freya said. "She's a beautiful girl, sweet as can be. My regulars love her. But she can't scene with just anybody. I don't know quite what happened with that ex of hers, but I do know it wasn't good. You're the only one I trust to give her what she needs without . . ." She let her sentence trail off with a sigh. "Let's just say, without potentially damaging her further."

Well, he sure hadn't been expecting that when he answered the phone. This sounded more like his friend Aiden's area of expertise. The man was brilliant at taking traumatized, broken subs and making them blossom. Just look at Aiden's fiancée, Olivia. She showed up at the Manor a fucking mess, but now? Not only were they deliriously happy together, but she also played a third in scenes with the other Manor Doms from time to time. Rafe fucking loved playing with her.

"Don't think I'm saying no," he said, though that's absolutely what he wanted to do. "But I'm not exactly known for using kid gloves with my subs." The Manor's founding partners had brought Rafe in for the guests who liked to play rough. *Really* rough.

"Have you looked at her limits?" He could practically hear the haughty expression on her face.

Their applications were almost twenty pages long, and he hadn't bothered skimming past page two. Holding in a sigh, he skipped past several pages, scrolling down to the start of the limits section. Pages thirteen through nineteen contained a comprehensive checklist, where potential subs could rate various activities from one (a hard limit, never to be tried) to five (which was basically the sub saying, "Yes, *please*.")

"Oh," he said as he scanned through the pages. There were only a handful of ones and more fives than he'd ever seen during his time at the Manor. "I see."

"Yes, I thought you might."

Nell Beaumont liked to play *hard*. No kid gloves required after all.

"She hasn't told me much, so this is all speculation," Freya said, "but I think she was in a full-time M/s relationship. And I think the guy was an abusive piece of shit."

Rafe cringed. It was so easy for an unscrupulous Dom to abuse his power—*especially* in those full-time Master/slave scenarios where the sub gave up the ability to use a safeword.

"It's clear she needs, shall we say, a heavy hand. Nothing less will satisfy her. But anytime someone approaches her at my club, she panics." Her voice turned sad, even pitying. "I found her hyperventilating in the bathroom once, though of course she refused to tell me what happened. I had to find out from one of my other employees."

It was enough to thaw even his stone-cold heart. But he still didn't understand what he could do about it. "Why would she be any different with me?"

"Nell trusts me. Entirely."

No surprise there. Freya had collected a number of subs since opening Valhalla's doors, of various sexualities and gender identities, hovering over them like an overprotective mother hen.

"If I tell her she can trust you, she'll believe me. And I do trust you. I know you inside and out, and I'm telling you, this girl needs you."

Rafe was flattered as all hell, no doubt about that. If he was being honest, though, this sounded like his own personal nightmare. Maybe if he could tag-team with Aiden, the other man could do all the emotional baggage shit, leaving Rafe to handle the fun parts. Then it wouldn't be so bad.

But no, that would never work. Freya barely knew Aiden. She'd never trust a near-stranger with this new girl of hers.

When he didn't answer after several seconds, Freya made a low noise of frustration. "Jesus, Rafe, I'd do it myself if I could give her what she needs. But you know I can't go that hard. Do this for me. Please."

"All right, all right." He rolled his eyes. "I'll do it. I'll have Zach send the acceptance letter as soon as the real application comes in." Zach Potter was the Manor's receptionist, though that job title didn't even begin to cover all his duties. The whole place would fall apart without him. Rafe would shoot him a text as soon as he and Freya got off the phone.

"Thank you." Such profound relief filled those whispered words, Rafe felt a pang of guilt in the pit of his stomach for denying her for so long.

Unable to help himself, he asked, "What is it about her? I've never heard you get this worked up over one of your girls."

She stayed quiet for a long time, and Rafe knew her well enough not to press. She'd answer him when she was ready to and not a moment before—if she chose to answer at all.

When at last Freya spoke, there was a slight tremor in her voice. "She reminds me of Ian."

The unspoken words were clear enough: *I couldn't save Ian. But I can save her.*

Well, didn't that just make him feel all warm and fuzzy inside. If he fucked this up, it would be like Freya losing her husband all over again. And it would all be his fault.

No pressure or anything.

CHAPTER 3

Nell

A n enormous black sedan picked Nell up at the airport in Manchester, New Hampshire, the driver stowing her shabby duffel in the trunk before whisking her northward. Nestled in the soft leather of the back seat, she stared out the window as the boat-like car carried her deeper and deeper into Vermont's Green Mountains.

Man, this place was remote as fuck. Mistress Freya told her Fairford Manor was in the middle of nowhere, but she'd seriously been in the car for almost three hours at this point. She hadn't seen anything but trees for the last thirty minutes or more, and not so much as a single billboard since they crossed into the state.

Not that she minded. Vermont in October had to be just about the most beautiful thing she'd seen in her life. Some of the leaf colors looked almost too spectacular to be real.

"Not long to go now," the driver said, seeming to sense her restlessness. She looked up in time to see him smile at her in the rearview mirror.

Nell returned his smile, wondering for about the twentieth time how the Manor made any money. She did her fair share of snooping after Mistress Freya got her to fill out that long-ass application, and the place was supposed to be super fucking fancy. Like, antique furniture, world-class dungeon, extravagant food, and expensive wine fancy. Plus, Rafe (her "host" apparently) would be with her almost 24/7 if she wanted. And she even got this free ride to and from the airport—a six-hour round trip in a Lexus for Christ's sake.

Yet her stay only cost a little over two hundred dollars a night? Even if you didn't count all the other expensive shit, that meant Rafe would be working for under ten bucks an hour. Something about this definitely didn't add up.

A niggling little suspicion started to form in the back of her mind, but before she could solidify it into actual thought, great stone pillars appeared around a bend in the road. She sat up a little straighter, craning her neck to get a better view of the open wrought iron gates. What was this place, a fucking castle?

"Here we are." The driver sounded downright cheerful as he turned on his blinker. Probably glad to finally get rid of her. She'd never been very good at small talk, so the guy had to be bored out of his mind. The sorry state of her luggage didn't exactly imply she'd be a good tipper, either, though she intended to prove otherwise.

As they passed through the gates, Nell's breath caught in her throat. "Goddamn," she muttered, her eyes wide. It wasn't a castle after all, though there were probably castles smaller than this place. The mansion was a pristine white, as if not a single speck of dirt ever dared to touch it. Three stories high, it had about half a million windows, each with black shutters and an old-fashioned crisscross pattern in the windowpanes. A huge farmer's porch stretched across most of the front.

"Pretty, isn't it?" the driver said as he wound his way down the long driveway.

She made a sound sort of like, "*Chyeah*," as she turned in her seat, trying to take everything else in. A beautiful, perfectly mowed lawn stretched out from the house to the front gates, with a copse of pine trees off to one side. Beyond the lawn and house, dense forest surrounded them, all the intense oranges, reds, and yellows of the autumn leaves interspersed with the occasional deep green of more pines.

Yeah, no fucking way did this place cost under five hundred a night.

Hell, for all she knew, it could be a thousand. If the situation got any fishier, it would reek like all those giant fish they tossed around at Pike Place in Seattle, where she grew up.

Had Mistress Freya secretly paid for the bulk of her stay? Or maybe her boss got her some sort of friend-of-a-friend pity discount; it was clear the Mistress and Rafe were close. At the end of the day, though, there was only one question that actually mattered.

Did she care?

Her pride said yes, but her libido was ready to bitch-slap her pride in the face.

"Alrighty then," the driver said, pulling into a parking spot and turning off the car. "Here at last." He hopped out as she started to open her own door, pulling it the rest of the way open for her.

Climbing out of the back seat, she stood beside her driver, whose name she seemed to have forgotten, though it definitely started with a D. Dane, maybe? Or Dean? They stood on either side of the door, staring up at the colossal house.

"Hope you don't take this the wrong way," Dane/Dean said, his voice gentle and kind, "but you don't seem as excited as the other girls I drove up here. Everything okay?"

Warmth spread from the center of her chest, and she felt her lips curving up. After all the shit she went through with Micah, it felt good to have people looking out for her. If only she'd listened to the people looking out for her back then. "Yes, everything's good," she promised, looking Dane/Dean in the eyes so he could see she meant it.

"So long as you're sure," he said, his own eyes crinkling at the corners. "Because I'll be driving right back through Manchester anyway. If you decide you've changed your mind, makes no difference to me if you're in the car or not."

Okay, Dane/Dean deserved an extra big tip. And for her to know his actual name. "Thank you. Really." She put a hand on his upper arm, giving it a grateful squeeze. "I'm actually really excited to be here. I promise. I've just got a lot on my mind." Then, doing her best to look sufficiently chagrined, she asked, "And I'm so sorry, but what was your name again?"

He seemed pleased to be asked, rather than insulted she hadn't remembered. "Dale."

Damn, *so* close.

"Well, thank you, Dale. I really appreciate you looking out for me." She reached into her little fake leather purse, pulling out her wallet. She'd stopped at an ATM in the Tampa airport, pretty much draining the last of her savings. The rest of her laptop money and most of her emergency fund already went to the Manor and Spirit Airlines, and that was *with* the pity discount.

Peeling off five twenties, she held them out to Dale. A hundred dollars was a good tip, right? Or maybe it wasn't for such a long drive. She considered reaching back in for more when Dale held up his hands. "That won't be necessary. The gratuity has already been taken care of."

Of course it had. "Consider this a bonus, then," she said, pushing the wad of cash into his hand, "for being awesome."

Dale grinned as he slipped the bills into his pocket. When he removed his hand a moment later, he held a business card between two fingers. "You need a ride back to the airport before Saturday, you give me a call, okay? Anytime, day or night."

She accepted the card, looking down at the cartoon picture of a uniformed driver leaning against the hood of a black car. "Thank you." She put it in a side pocket of her purse, then gave Dale a final smile. "But you really don't have to worry about me. I'll see you on Saturday."

"Looking forward to it." Popping the trunk, he held up her duffle bag. "Help you inside with this?"

"Oh no, I'm fine." Nell took the bag from him, slipping the strap over her shoulder. "Have a safe trip back."

With a little salute, he climbed into his car. As he backed out of his parking spot and started down the long driveway, Nell pulled the business card out of her purse, wrapping her fingers around it. She wasn't stranded here. If she hated it or she freaked the fuck out the second Rafe touched her . . .

But no, that wasn't going to happen. For the thousandth time since that surprise meeting in her boss's office a month ago, she reminded herself this was one of Mistress Freya's mentees. One of the people she trusted most in the world.

Rafe wasn't going to be Micah 2.0.

Please, God, don't be like Micah. Don't even look like him.

Her chest tightened at the thought, her fear like a fist around her heart. But she took a long, slow breath, letting it out through her mouth. Micah could fuck right off; no way would she let the mere memory of him ruin this for her. Time to put on her big girl panties and go inside.

Squaring her shoulders, Nell walked up the flagstone path like a soldier marching into battle. She admired the fall decorations as she went by—mums of every color, enormous pumpkins, dozens of gourds, all arranged artfully enough to belong on the cover of a magazine. But she didn't let herself slow down. If this happened at all, it had to be *now*.

More pumpkins lined the wide steps up to the porch, paired with gorgeous black metal lanterns, the thick pillar candles inside already lit for the night. Nell glanced down the length of the farmer's porch as she crossed it, taking in the assortment of rocking chairs and cushioned loveseats. This place seriously might be a dream come true.

When she pushed her way through one of the double front doors, her mouth dropped open the tiniest bit. Jesus, it was even fancier than she expected. White marble tiles with dark gray veining stretched across the entryway, gleaming in the late afternoon sunlight. A wide, curved staircase waited at the other end of the lobby with a dark, polished wood banister and what looked like an antique stair runner, like something out of an old movie. Her gaze traveled up to the crystal chandelier hanging from the vaulted ceiling. A legit fucking crystal chandelier.

"Holy shit," she muttered, clutching her shabby duffel bag a little closer to her side. This place screamed Aubrey Hepburn and Grace Kelly. She should be wearing Dior and dripping in diamonds, not wandering into the place in her own special brand of thrift-store chic.

"Welcome, Ms. Beaumont."

Nell shrieked, whipping toward the unknown voice with a racing heart.

"Shit, sorry!" A vested and bow-tied man in his twenties stood behind the reception desk, holding out both hands in a placating gesture. "I didn't mean to scare you."

A blush crept up her neck to her face. "Sorry," she said back, not quite able to meet his eyes. "I, uh . . . I startle really easily." That was the understatement of the century. Compliments of her years living with Micah.

Surprises from him had never been a good thing.

She only hoped her fight-or-flight response would calm down eventually, but it was as strong now as the day she finally left that asshole. Forcing herself to smile, she crossed the marble tiles toward the front desk. The slender man behind it had a deep crease between his brows and guilt shadowing his eyes. "Really, it's not your fault," she assured him. "I didn't see you there."

That crease between his brows smoothed away, and he smiled. "I appreciate that, Ms. Beaumont. So, accidental jump scares aside, how was your trip?"

"*Long*," she said, slumping theatrically. She left for the airport at five that morning and was too amped up to sleep on the plane or in the car. "But uneventful. I'm so glad to finally be here. And please, it's Nell."

His smile grew a little less customer service, a little more genuine. "Zach Potter. We spoke on the phone last month."

Oh, she definitely remembered who Zach was. She'd read the acceptance letter he sent so many times the paper tore along one of the folds. "It's good to have a face to go with the voice." She tried to make her own smile as warm and kind as Zach's, but she was too on edge. Where was Rafe? When was all the Dom shit going to start? Perhaps she should've included on her application how calm an exact schedule made her feel . . . and how anxiety inducing deviations to that schedule were.

Zach seemed to sense her unease, probably from the way her gaze kept flicking over toward the stairs. "Rafe is waiting for you up in your room," he told her. "He doesn't expect you for several more minutes, so we have plenty of time to get you checked in."

Some of the tension left her shoulders, and she had a feeling her smile looked a little less like that of a deranged psychopath. "Thank you," she said, trying to show him with her eyes how much she meant it. "I don't know what I'm so nervous about. It's not like I haven't done this before. Probably just sleep deprivation."

Yeah, that was a giant fucking lie. But she didn't need other people knowing—or even guessing at—her private business.

If Zach could tell she was full of shit, he chose not to show it. Instead, he helped her get checked in, having her sign a liability agreement about the risks of unprotected sex and the various elements of BDSM, a multi-page consent form listing all the limits from her application, and finally a list of the house rules.

He gave her a moment to shoot off a final text to Mistress Freya, confirming her safe arrival at the Manor, before locking her phone in a safe under the desk. She knew coming in that any sort of recording device was banned on Manor property, and she certainly understood. Nell wouldn't want a video of herself deep in a scene showing up on the internet. But still, she couldn't help feeling bereft without it.

Her fingers found Dale's card in her purse again. "I understand the whole no phones or cameras thing," she started, "but if I need to make a call—"

"There's a phone right here you can use anytime you want," Zach said, gesturing toward the front desk. "Or if you need privacy, I'd be happy to let you use the phone in my office." He hooked a thumb over his shoulder, toward the open door behind him.

The knot of anxiety in her chest loosened enough for her to take a deep breath. "Perfect. Thank you." She wasn't stranded here. These people were nothing like Micah. Everything was on her terms now.

Her terms, her choice, her rules.

With another deep breath, she gave Zach a stronger smile and said, "I'm ready to meet Rafe now if that's okay."

"Of course. Your suite is right at the top of the stairs."

Nell resisted the urge to hide her old duffel bag and cheap purse from Zach's view as she crossed the lobby. She may not be as fancy as the other people who came here, but she refused to act ashamed. If this duffel was good enough to carry her few remaining possessions out of Micah's house and across the country, it was good enough for Fairford fucking Manor.

Brushing her fingertips along the smooth, curving banister, Nell climbed the stairs with her back straight and her head held high. Some primal survival instinct deep inside yelled at her to run, to not go down this road again. It wasn't worth the risk. Better to be celibate and alone for the rest of her life than to gamble on even a fraction of her history repeating itself.

But her pussy seemed to be calling the shots, cause the next thing she knew she stood in front of her suite's door. Before she could talk herself out of it, she twisted the knob and shoved the door open, stepping inside.

Relief enveloped her whole body the moment she saw him, the feeling so intense she nearly sagged against the doorframe. He couldn't have looked less like Micah if he actively tried.

Unlike Micah's shoulder-length, dirty blond hair, Rafe's was short and dark. The dim lighting made it impossible to tell if it was an incredibly deep brown or black. His perfectly trimmed beard and strong jaw were the exact opposite of her ex's smooth, pointed face. Tattoos started at his right wrist and disappeared under the sleeve of his T-shirt, the wings of some sort of large bird and part of a wolf visible from where she stood. Micah despised tattoos and had often called the one wrapping around her thigh vulgar and classless.

And Rafe was clearly no stranger to the gym, while her ex had a slender, wiry build.

Shouldn't she be afraid? Micah hadn't had any issues manhandling her when he wanted to, and this guy looked like he could snap her in half.

And yet, there wasn't a trace of fear left in her. Not once she looked into his gray-green eyes. That was the biggest difference of all. He looked stern, strong, intimidating . . . but not cruel. Not at all cruel. She hadn't recognized that look in Micah when she first met him. But she sure as hell recognized the lack of it now.

Nell would've expected some sort of command by now. Instead, he continued studying her from his spot near the fireplace, his full lips parted slightly, his beautiful eyes brimming with interest. As if he was waiting to see what she would do.

She closed her eyes for one second, two—only long enough to draw a fortifying breath into her lungs. Then she let the straps of her two bags slide down her arm, depositing them on the floor beside her. The door swung shut as she moved across the room, until she was close enough to the fire to feel its heat on her bare legs. And as her new Dom watched in silence, she dropped gracefully to her knees on the hearthrug, hands resting on her spread thighs.

"Master Rafe." Her voice stuck on the words, but she forced them out anyway. "Please instruct me on how best to serve you."

CHAPTER 4
Rafe

Rafe's breath caught in his lungs. No one had called him that in a very, *very* long time. God, he'd almost forgotten what it felt like.

Damn did it feel good coming from her lips. Especially since Nell was even prettier in person than in her photo, with her dark eyes and hair practically glowing in the firelight. She was taller than he expected, only an inch or two shy of six feet if he had to guess, with legs that went on for days. The edges of a black and blue tattoo were visible on her right thigh, peeking out from the hem of her rose-pink dress. Christ, he wanted to know what it felt like to have those thighs wrapped around his head, squeezing him with their obvious strength.

But Rafe wasn't even close to ready for that level of address again. Fuck, he wasn't sure he would ever be able to let another woman call him that. Not with how it ended last time.

"I don't allow anyone without my collar around their neck to call me Master." He thought he'd sounded sufficiently calm—even gentle, for him at least—but she shrunk in on herself like he had shouted the words in her face. Head down, shoulders hunched, as if she expected blows.

Christ, where was Aiden when he needed him?

But no, he was on his own and he damn well knew it. Freya would have his balls if he tried to foist the girl off on someone else. So he'd have to do the next best thing—channel his inner good guy and figure out WWAD?

Actually, he knew exactly what Aiden would do. He watched it happen last year on Olivia's first day at the Manor, when the girl started hyperventilating down in the dungeon. Aiden would get down on her level and hold her, whispering calming shit until she was all smiles and sunshine.

Just the idea of it had him grinding his teeth hard enough to make his jaw ache. No way could he pull that off. He was nothing like Aiden.

And, he reminded himself, this girl wasn't Olivia. Freya had sent her to *him*. So he was going to do things his way.

"Nell," he said, doing his best to sound stern but not angry. Her entire body flinched at the sound of his voice. Holding in a frustrated sigh, he cupped her chin in his hand—not hard enough to hurt, but with enough force that she'd know better than to try pulling away. "I want you to look at me and sit up straight for me."

Rafe could feel her trembling. It had a small part of him reconsidering the whole hug-her-and-say-sappy-shit plan. But then she slowly unfurled from the ball she'd curled herself into, straightening her spine and lifting her chin. The last thing she did was open her eyes, gazing directly into his.

There was so much pain in those big brown eyes, he almost took a step back. But she deserved better than that. She'd earned it, by being brave enough to come to the Manor, to do as he said no matter how hard it was for her.

So he held her gaze, studying the rings of darker brown in her irises, similar to the rings inside a tree. With that haunted look in her eyes, it was as if each ring represented another terrible memory instead of another year of her life.

"Let's get one thing perfectly clear from the start." Rafe's voice came out a little more gravelly than usual. "You'll never have to wonder if I'm upset with you. If you do something I don't like, I'll ask you to fix it. As long as you do what you're told, everything will be fine. I'll never be angry with you or punish you for making an honest mistake or for not being able to read my mind."

Nell's brows drew together, as if she didn't quite understand what he was saying. "But . . ." She trailed off, like she wasn't sure she was allowed to voice her confusion.

"But?" Rafe prompted.

"But if you don't punish me for messing up, what *will* you punish me for? Isn't punishing me the whole point?"

Fucking hell, Freya was right. That ex of hers really did a number on her. "Dominance and submission isn't about punishing you for every little mistake you make." He realized he was stroking her cheek with his thumb. How long had that been going on? Forcing his hand to still, he said, "It's about mutual satisfaction. About both of us trusting the other to give us what we need."

The sheer level of bewilderment on her lovely face would've been comical if it wasn't so fucking heart-wrenching. Unable to stop himself, he brushed his thumb along her bottom lip, and she snapped her gaping mouth closed.

"I'm sensing," Rafe started, releasing her face at last, "you may need a bit of a reeducation in what a good D/s relationship should look like. Let's see if I can help with that." Reaching out to her, he stood perfectly still until she tentatively put her hands in his. He pulled her to her feet, leading her away from the fireplace and over to the sofa. "Before we get started, let's get you out of this dress."

Grabbing the hem, he went to lift it over her head, expecting her to raise her arms. Instead, the heel of her palm came crashing down onto his wrist, knocking his hand away. A second later, her other hand lashed out toward his face.

"What the fuck?" Rafe shouted as he jerked out of the way, his reflexes the only thing saving him from a broken nose.

For a second, it looked like she was gearing up for an actual fight, stance wide and hands up by her face. But then her instincts faded away, and her arms dropped limply at her sides. Nell went full deer in head-lights, eyes wide and unfocused, body utterly still. He was pretty sure she wasn't even breathing.

"Hey," he said, cupping her chin again, harder than last time. His fingertips dug into the soft flesh of her cheeks. "Eyes on me, kitten."

Using Freya's nickname for the girl seemed to snap her out of it, and she blinked, suddenly looking at him instead of through him. He'd have to remember to thank his former mentor for that little tip.

"I'm sorry, Sir," Nell said, fear making her voice shake. "Please, I didn't mean—"

"You're not in trouble." When she started to protest, he tightened his grip. "*Look at me.* You are *not* in trouble."

She stared into his eyes, hers large and round. "I hit you." Her voice was so small, so confused.

"I surprised you, and you reacted instinctively. And your instincts were flawless." His wrist hurt like a motherfucker. Her body knew exactly which steps to take to protect her, like she'd practiced until it became muscle memory. "Do you study martial arts?"

"Self-defense classes," she answered. "I'm so sorry. I know you weren't trying to hurt me, but my brain kind of short-circuited and I—"

"From now on, I only want you to apologize when you've actually done something wrong." He loosened his grip, but couldn't bring himself to let go of her. "Do you understand?"

"But, if hitting you isn't wrong . . ." She swallowed. "How am I supposed to know what is?"

Christ almighty, she looked so fucking lost. Like he set her loose in the middle of a labyrinth and demanded she find her way out on the first try.

"Your ex made it hard to tell, didn't he?" Rafe asked, surprised by the softness in his own voice.

Humiliation flashed through her eyes, but she didn't look away. "Impossible," she whispered.

"How about this." He'd have to revise his plan on the fly. "You don't apologize at all unless I tell you to. That way you can learn to tell the difference again."

The faint lines around her lovely brown eyes softened, and she gave him a smile that could light up a room. Hell, it could light a whole fucking stadium. Her picture *definitely* hadn't done her justice. "Thank you, Sir."

Rafe stared at her for a few more seconds, mesmerized, before he managed to get out, "You're welcome. Will you take your dress off for me now?"

The smile disappeared in an instant.

His mind raced as he tried to figure out what to do. Punish her for not obeying? Force her to either take it off or use her safeword?

No, none of that felt remotely okay to him. If whatever went down with her ex made her too afraid to be touched, he sure as fuck wasn't going to make it worse. She could always go back to Freya and try again later.

After a way-too-long pause, he settled on saying, "Tell me why this scares you so much."

Hugging her arms over her stomach, she said, "There's something I left out of my application. Something I should've put in there. I'm sor —" At his arched brow, she let the apology trail off.

"That application may be twenty goddamn pages long, but that doesn't mean you can fit every single thing about yourself into it." Rafe's tone left absolutely no room for argument. "You're not going to be in trouble. Just tell me what it is."

She hugged herself a little tighter, but then forced her arms to her sides, her hands curled into fists. Screwing her eyes shut, Nell blurted, "I have scars." The tension drained out of her muscles as soon as the words were out, and she opened her eyes. "A lot of them. No one has seen them since . . . not since Micah."

Micah. That must be the piece of shit ex. He wanted to fucking pulverize the man.

"Is Micah the one who gave you the scars?" Murder bled through his tone, and he damn well knew it. He couldn't even bring himself to feel bad when she flinched.

Her gaze slid away, resting somewhere near his shoulder. "Some of them. *Most* of them."

Rafe started to ask what she meant, but then closed his mouth without making a sound. He thought he had a pretty damn good idea.

"There's a quote I heard once," he said, striving for a calm he didn't feel, "though I don't remember where. It went something like this: Scars show you where you've been. But they have nothing to do with where you're going."

Her gaze flew to his, something new flaring in her eyes. He couldn't tell what it meant, but he wanted more. That look . . . that *burn* . . .

So fucking beautiful. It was intoxicating.

"And if you're worried your scars will bother me," he added, sliding his hand up into her hair. "Don't. You're beautiful, Nell. Every single inch of you. I don't have to see the rest of you to know, but I'm happy to prove it to you whenever you're ready."

She leaned into his hand, eyes closing, mouth parting on a sigh. Then she raised her arms up toward the ceiling.

Rafe let out a low hum of satisfaction. "Good girl." Before fear could change her mind, he grasped the hem of her dress and pulled, slipping it up over her head and tossing it onto a chair.

Fuck, she was breathtaking. She wore a lacy push up bra and matching thong, the same dusky pink color as her dress. The skin from her breasts to her upper thighs clearly never saw the light of day, the color several shades lighter than the rest of her body. His gaze traveled lower, to her long, muscular legs, where a large black and blue butterfly wrapped around her upper thigh.

Rafe walked slowly around her, taking it all in. There were several raised scars between her lower back and upper thighs—crisscrossing lines that probably came from a cane or whip wielded with too heavy a hand. He'd have to show her what those implements felt like in the hands of a master.

As he moved around the other side, his gaze zeroed in on another set of thick, raised lines on her right hip. But these weren't chaotic like the others; a glance told him they'd been placed there in a specific pattern. His steps faltered when he realized what it was.

A capital M, capital I, and the beginning of a C.

Jesus fucking Christ. Micah clearly wasn't only a piece of shit. He was a fucking psychopath.

"Remind me," Rafe said, doing everything in his power to keep the anger and revulsion out of his voice. "What's the safeword you put in your application? It was a bird, wasn't it?"

"Sparrow, Sir."

He could hear the frown in her voice. Circling around to her front, he peered into her troubled face. "What's wrong?"

Nell chewed on her bottom lip for a moment, as if unsure she wanted to answer. But then she gazed into his face, and his commanding look seemed to sway her decision. "That was always my safeword . . . *before*."

It was obvious that she meant *before Micah*.

"Is it okay if I change it? I don't want to go back to where I was." That burning *something* was back in her eyes, and he couldn't tear his gaze away. "Like that quote you said about my scars. I want to go somewhere new. Somewhere better."

"New Dom, new safeword, new you?" Rafe said, one corner of his mouth lifting.

She blushed beautifully but didn't look away. "That sounds stupid, doesn't it?"

"No." Wrapping his arms around her, Rafe claimed her mouth at last—something he'd been longing to do since she walked through the door. She stiffened for about half a second, then went almost liquid in his arms, her lips parting eagerly to allow his tongue entrance.

Fuck, she smelled good, like sun-ripened peaches. And she tasted so minty and fresh, he wanted to devour her. With one hand gripping her hair right at the scalp, the other digging into the naked flesh of her ass, he kissed her like a man starved.

When at last he pulled away, she leaned toward him, eyes still closed, chasing the kiss. "It doesn't sound stupid at all," he ground out, voice low and saturated with lust. They needed to get the whole safeword thing sorted out before they could go any further. "Pick whatever word you want."

She opened her eyes slowly, dazedly blinking. "Whatever word I want?" There was a soft, dreamy quality to her voice that made his mind race with possibilities. If he could do that to her with a kiss, he couldn't wait to see what happened when he fucked her.

"Having trouble focusing, little girl?" he asked, hearing the boast in his own voice, and not caring in the least. "Let's figure this one thing out, and then I promise I'll finish what I just started."

A shiver ran through her whole body at his words. Nell glanced around the room, urgency in her gaze as she searched for inspiration for the new safeword.

"How about butterfly?" Rafe suggested, brushing his thumb over the tattoo on her thigh.

They both went utterly still at the exact same moment. The ink covered a series of raised parallel lines—obvious self-harm scars. Apparently he'd been right about what Nell meant when she said only *most* of her scars came from her ex.

"Never mind," he hurried to say. "Let's figure out something else."

"No, I like it," she whispered, staring down at the intricate blue and black tattoo. "I went to a tattoo parlor with a friend a few weeks after I started college. The artist had a drawing of this with her available designs. I remember thinking how good it would feel, turning something ugly into something so beautiful. Just like a caterpillar turning into a butterfly."

He wanted to tell her again that she was beautiful. That he hadn't been able to take his eyes off her from the moment she entered the room. But then her fingertips brushed over the half-carved name on her hip, and the words stuck in his throat.

"I wish it was that easy. I wish I could wrap myself up in every choice I ever made, good or bad. And when it all comes undone, there's a whole new beautiful me." She finished on a whisper.

Rafe found himself absolutely speechless for the first time in his life. How long had he been working toward something similar? Trying to take all the jagged, fucked up pieces of his past and reform them into something good and right.

"Like you said before—new Dom, new safeword, new me." She raised her gaze to his and smiled. "It's perfect, Sir."

Realizing he was just standing there, gaping at her like an idiot, he forced out a stilted, "Well then. Now that's settled." He needed to get this scene back on track, and fast. Taking hold of her, he yanked her down over his lap as he sat on the sofa, smiling at her surprised laugh. "Time to start your reeducation. I'm going to ask you some questions. I need to understand you better so I can make sure I give you what you need. They're not going to be easy questions, but if you're a good girl and answer well"—he cupped her pussy over her skimpy thong—"I'll give you a reward."

She squirmed under his hand and let out a long, harsh breath. Not surprising if she'd been celibate for as long as Freya suspected.

When he pulled his hand away, her groan of frustration made his cock ache. This was going to be fun.

"What happens if I don't?" she asked, and he had a feeling anticipation laced her voice now, not fear.

Rafe brought his hand down across the very center of her perfectly round bottom, hard enough to genuinely hurt. "If you're a bad girl and don't answer honestly, I'll punish you."

Her breath hitched, and her ass and thighs clenched together so tight, it was a wonder she didn't get a cramp. So Freya was right; she sent him a pain slut.

He made a mental note to send the woman some flowers.

"Which, I suspect, you'll also like," he said, letting some of his amusement slip into his voice. "So how about this. You don't have to answer any questions you don't want to. But if you don't answer enough of them, you don't get to come. I'll be the only one getting any pleasure tonight, and we can try something else tomorrow."

A half groan, half moan escaped her as she buried her face in the sofa cushion. He could tell the idea of being edged all night was as scintillating as it was horrifying. Goddamn, he wanted to fuck her, and he wanted to do it *right the fuck now*. "I'll be a good girl, Sir. I swear."

"I'll hold you to that." He gave her ass a harsh squeeze before lifting his hand away. "Let's start with an easy one. When did you figure out you're submissive?"

She hesitated for only a moment before she spoke. "My sophomore year of college."

"What happened?"

"I walked in on my roommate and her boyfriend fucking. He'd handcuffed her to the headboard." Her voice deepened with lust when she added, "I started fantasizing about him doing the same thing to me. It was pretty obvious the handcuffing part did it for me, because I thought he was a total douche."

Rafe slid his hand back to her pussy, letting a single finger slip inside. He pumped it in and out of her slowly, taking his time to gather her slick moisture on his finger. "Was your first experience with the roommate's douche boyfriend or someone else?"

Instead of answering, she clenched her pussy around his finger, as if trying to draw him in deeper. When he removed it entirely rather than give her what she wanted, she groaned and started talking. "Definitely not him. I hated his guts. It was a different guy I met at a party. He wasn't into it at all, but he agreed to spank me and tie me up while he fucked me if I sucked him off first. I was probably gonna do that anyway, so it seemed like a fair enough trade."

Rafe frowned down at the woman draped over his thighs. That wasn't exactly an auspicious beginning to her kink journey. And he already knew the story didn't get better from there.

But she answered his question honestly, and that deserved another reward. Brushing his finger softly over her clit, he used her moisture to pleasure her. Her fingers dug into the sofa cushion as he continued giving her the lightest of touches—only enough to make her ache for more.

When he pulled away, she let out a frustrated huff of air but didn't complain. "Good girl. So what came next? More trades with vanilla frat boys? Or did you find someone better suited to your needs?"

"Definitely no more vanilla guys," she said, a hard finality in her voice. "He wouldn't spank me even close to hard enough. And I didn't come when he fucked me. I don't think it occurred to him to care or even try. Total waste of time."

Something that felt very much like pride swelled inside his chest. Why he should feel pride for this girl he just met, over a decision she'd made almost twenty years ago, was quite beyond him. But he couldn't think of another word to describe the feeling.

"For a while, all I did was read kinky books. I learned as much about it all as I could, memorized the lingo." She shot him a saucy little wink over her shoulder. "Had about a billion orgasms. You know how it is."

He gave her a few mild spanks for her sass and tried not to think too deeply about her masturbating for weeks on end to a string of dirty novels. Admittedly, he wasn't particularly successful.

"I met a guy named Brian online a few months later. He was older— early thirties when we got together. Great job, nice condo in L.A., expensive car. I liked that he had his shit together. He knew exactly what he was doing. He promised to teach me how to be the perfect submissive. He's the one I was with when I picked sparrow as a safeword."

The frown was right back on Rafe's face. Age gaps were common enough in kinky *and* vanilla couples, but he'd never approved of grown-ass adults getting into relationships with teenagers, legal or not. The Manor didn't even allow anyone under twenty-one to apply, thank God. And to keep to his own personal code, he never chose guests under twenty-five. The idea of being with someone whose brain wasn't even done developing repulsed him.

"And how long were you with Brian the stockbroker?" he asked.

She laughed. It was a soft, beautiful sound, and he wanted to hear it again. "Good guess, but he actually did something else in finance. I don't even remember what it was. He never really got into the details, and to be honest, I never cared." She shrugged, her shoulder blades shifting under her golden skin. Rafe found himself tracing the protruding bones with a fingertip. "We were together a little over five years."

Not exactly surprising. Once Brian got his claws in her, he wouldn't have wanted to let her go. Nell would have been easy to manipulate and groom at that age.

Applying a little more pressure to her clit, Rafe kept rubbing in what he knew were excruciatingly slow circles. She pressed back against his hand, searching for more, but he refused to give it to her. She'd have to earn it first.

"What was your relationship like?" Rafe asked, moving his hand down to rest on her thigh, covering the patchwork of scars there.

She squirmed again, her belly pressing against his cock, making it strain even more to be free. "I don't know." There was a note of sulkiness in her voice. "Fine, I guess."

Without hesitation, Rafe brought his hand cracking down against her ass, five times on each cheek. She was gasping by the time his hand returned to her thigh.

"Want to try that one again? Or would you rather move on or use your safeword?" If she really had been in a full-time power exchange scenario, she'd need frequent reminding that she always had a choice. "It's up to you."

She'd tensed up during her punishment, but slowly relaxed against the sofa cushions. "At first, I thought he was perfect," she admitted. "He understood things about me I didn't even understand about myself. He had a bit of a temper, but I *liked* the pain, so I didn't consider it a problem. And after, he always bought me the most amazing things. Designer clothes, nice jewelry, expensive makeup, perfume. That sort of stuff."

"Did he ever go too far?"

She was quiet for several seconds—which was all the answer he needed, really.

"What happened?"

"He did something to piss me off. Went on a business trip without telling me, I think." Her voice was quieter than it had been. "He told me to be waiting at his place when he got back, but I was mad, so I went out with some friends instead. He was at my apartment when I got home."

He definitely knew where this was going. "Did he hit you?"

"Yes." She breathed the word.

"A lot?"

That time, all she could do was nod.

Rafe closed his eyes, taking several calming breaths before asking, "What did he buy you to make up for that?"

"An Audi." She sounded ashamed to admit it.

More like she was ashamed to admit it worked.

"It's not your fault," Rafe told her, squeezing her thigh, feeling the thin lines against his skin. "You were practically still a kid. He knew exactly how to manipulate you." And fuck it all, this was the guy *before* Micah.

"That's no excuse." Fuck, she was crying. He hated making women cry by mistake. It only brought him pleasure when it was intentional. "My friends told me to sell the car and leave his ass. And they were the same age as me."

"It's always easier to make a good judgment call when you're not in the situation yourself." He gave her leg a couple of awkward pats, wishing he knew how to soothe her properly. "And your dynamic with Brian already involved physical pain—something most of your friends probably also didn't understand. No wonder the lines got blurred."

Gathering some of her moisture on his thumb, he started rubbing harder circles against her clit, pumping his first two fingers in and out of her pussy at the same time. Nell must've figured out he stopped whenever she got greedy, because she stayed perfectly still. The only evidence he affected her at all came from her heavy breathing. She whimpered when he pulled away that time.

"What made you finally leave Brian?"

She drew in a long, shaky breath. "Micah."

Here we go, Rafe thought, not looking forward to this part of the story at all. "Where did you two meet?"

"An audition for a TV show pilot."

His brows shot upward. "You were an actress?"

"I was trying to be. That's why I went to college in L.A. I was a theater major."

She definitely hadn't put any of that info in her application. No way would he have forgotten a detail like that. "Did you get the part?"

Nell shook her head, and there was genuine remorse in her voice when she said, "The only parts I ever got were in theater productions at school. Micah started mentoring me after we met, giving me all sorts of advice I'm pretty sure now was bullshit. But he'd gotten a bunch of minor roles on TV shows, and even played a coffee shop owner with several lines in a Hallmark movie, so I figured he had to know what he was talking about. Besides, it's not like we were going for the same parts, so why would he want to sabotage me? And the sex was so fucking good at first . . ." She let out a long, frustrated sigh. "My auditions were all such big disasters, it wasn't even hard for Micah to convince me to give up."

Rage coursed through him with all the speed and fury of a wildfire. "That motherfucker manipulated you. He isolated you and fucked with your self-esteem so you'd do anything to keep his attention on you. That's what abusers do, the piece of shit."

Twisting around, Nell looked up at him, their gazes meeting. He almost looked away, not wanting to scare her, but the storm in his eyes didn't seem to frighten her at all. Perhaps because it wasn't directed at her. If anything, she looked calmer than she had since she walked into the room.

She settled back down over his thighs with a contented sigh. "It's okay. I know now I never would've made it in Hollywood anyway. I don't think I have the right temperament. You have to be willing to do anything to make it, to put yourself before everyone else, and I never could've done that." She shrugged. "Now I just have to figure out what the new dream should be. I don't want to be a bartender forever, but at least it got me on my feet again."

An idea spurred in Rafe's mind—or half an idea anyway. He needed to let it percolate before he knew if there was anything there. "So how did Micah get you away from Brian?" he asked, wanting to keep her talking.

"I'd been wanting more from Brian. More time. A stronger commitment to each other. I wanted him to take me as deep as we could possibly go into the whole BDSM thing . . . but it was always later, later, later. Then Micah came along, and he offered me everything I ever wanted. I fell for him so fast and hard, it's honestly embarrassing."

"He figured out exactly what you wanted to hear. Of course you fell for him."

With another little shrug, she said, "My friends and sister and parents despised him. My two best friends from high school and my sister Holly even staged an intervention once. They came down to L.A. when I wouldn't go home for Christmas. Jesus, why didn't I listen to them? Instead, I got so fucking mad. The shit I said to them . . ." Her sigh carried so many years of pain and regret, it made his chest ache. "I don't blame them for not talking to me after that. I wouldn't talk to me either. And, of course, there Micah was, convincing me they were just jealous."

"Like I said," Rafe started, clearing his throat when his voice caught, "that's what abusers do. Isolate and manipulate. If he could get you away from all the people who loved you and were looking out for you, the better his chances of keeping you under his thumb."

Her voice was so soft, he strained to hear her when she said, "Yeah, well, by the time I realized how bad things were, I was in so deep I didn't know how to get out." Her whole body trembled.

"Enough," Rafe said, hauling her up so she sat facing him, her legs straddling his thighs. "That's enough for now." Burying his hands in her hair, he held her still as his mouth crashed down over hers. He kissed her long and hard, the strokes of his tongue demanding, fingers tugging her hair enough to hurt.

Nell moaned into his mouth, rocking her pelvis along the bulge of his erection, clearly trying to spur him to do more.

When at last he pulled away, she was panting for breath. "Please don't stop," she begged, burying her hands in his hair as well, trying to pull his face closer to hers.

"Hands behind your back," he ordered, his voice like the crack of a whip. She reacted exactly as he wanted, jerking back, eyes flying open. Pulling away from him as if his skin burned her, she wrapped her fingers around her wrists at the small of her back. She opened her mouth to speak—presumably to apologize—but then snapped it closed with an audible click of her teeth.

"Good girl. You didn't know this, so you're not in trouble. But you're not to touch me unless I give you permission first. Do you understand?"

Her eyes stayed wide as she whispered, "Yes, Sir."

"Good. And you were such a good girl before, telling me more of your story than I ever could've asked for. For that, you get to pick what happens next. You've more than earned a reward. Tell me what you want."

"Spank me and fuck me." The words spilled out of her as a desperate plea. "As hard as you're willing to. *Please, Sir.* It's been so fucking long. I'm burning up from the inside out."

The intensity in her eyes stole his breath away. "That can be arranged."

CHAPTER 5

Nell

"Holy shit." The words left Nell's mouth before she even thought them. The dungeon now stretching out before her was that incredible. She'd seen so many different pieces of dungeon furniture in one place. Hell, she didn't even recognize all of them, and she was no stranger to a BDSM dungeon. She worked in one for fuck's sake.

Rafe moved up behind her, draping his hands over her shoulders, fingers splayed across her collarbones. "This is my sanctuary. My kingdom. The one place in the world where everything is as it should be." He tightened his grip until her breath caught. "I have a suspicion you'll feel exactly the same way."

She had a feeling he might be right. The low lighting and dark neutral colors, the uber sensual music, the cries of another sub as she was cropped nearby . . . the overwhelming sexiness of the man behind her. It all combined to make the most deliciously powerful aphrodisiac she'd ever come across.

It would be so easy to let go and lose herself in a place like this. And with a man like Rafe . . .

She still didn't understand what made her spill so many of her secrets upstairs. Something about the way he straddled the line between understanding and demanding, kindness and pain, seemed to force the words out of her like a truth potion. Especially after he saw the scars—saw them and didn't turn away with disgust.

"It's time for these to go," Rafe said, his hands trailing down her back to the clasp of her bra. Once he tossed that aside, he knelt behind her, sliding her panties down her legs inch by slow, painstaking inch, the brush of his fingers spreading goosebumps across her skin. As soon as her panties joined her discarded bra, he took her hand, the strength of his grip making it clear she had no choice in the matter. "I know just the place for you. This way."

Her heart raced as he led her across the dungeon, past endless types of spanking benches and bondage tables, stockades and pillories to twist subs into a myriad of positions, and cages of different sizes. Various tables and cabinets filled each section of the dungeon, stocked with every size, shape, color, and type of spanking, penetrating, restraining, and vibrating implement imaginable. Good God, this place had more toys than even the best sex stores.

When Rafe finally came to a halt, they stood in front of a black metal Saint Andrew's cross with matching padding. It towered over both of them, with deep crimson nylon cuffs dangling from four metal rings screwed into the beams. Rafe got to work moving the top two rings, screwing them back in at the highest possible position.

"Let's see if this is tall enough to stretch you out," he said, giving her long legs an appreciative leer.

Blushing with pleasure, Nell stepped forward, letting him guide her into position facing the cross. It stood at a slight angle, so she had no choice but to lean all her weight against it.

Rafe strapped her arms in first, letting loose a low growl of pleasure when she had to fully extend them to reach the wrist cuffs. He hurried to cuff her ankles to the lower corners, then stepped back to survey his work. "*Perfect*. This cross was made for you."

Another blush heating her skin, Nell closed her eyes and smiled. "Thank you, Sir." She couldn't imagine Micah or Brian ever saying something so kind to her. It made her feel more beautiful than she had in years.

Rafe moved up behind her, close enough for his breath to tickle the side of her neck. He gripped her ass, kneading it with his fingers, spreading her cheeks wide. "How long has it been since your last real spanking?" he asked, his lips brushing against her ear.

"Almost thirteen months, Sir." That's when she finally did it—packed her single bag and escaped from Micah for good.

"Mmm," he said, his fingers digging even harder into her flesh. "Such a long time. Your ass is going to be so soft and supple under my belt."

Nell's breath hitched, and she squeezed her eyes shut even tighter. She fucking *loved* the feel of leather biting into her skin. His T-shirt had hidden his belt from her view thus far, but she imagined what it would look like in his hand—a wide strip of worn leather with a gleaming silver buckle, doubled over in his fist. A moan slipped out before she could stop it.

"Does that excite you?" Rafe asked, one hand sliding lower, slipping into her wet folds. He pumped two fingers into her, then stopped. "That wasn't rhetorical, little girl."

"*Yes.*" The single word rushed out on a harsh exhale.

His fingers resumed their pumping motion. "What about it?"

"The pain," she said, choosing her words carefully. "But not only that. It's also that you want to give it to me. That it excites *you* when I'm a good girl and let you hurt me."

Rafe's other hand slipped around to her front, sliding between her pelvis and the Saint Andrew's cross. It was only a moment before he found her clit again, rubbing it with more pressure than he had upstairs.

"Please, Sir," she said, her breaths coming faster and faster with each passing moment, every muscle in her body taut. "*Please, please, please.*"

Both hands sped up, rubbing and finger fucking her until she couldn't think straight, until she was about to tumble off the edge. *Any . . . second . . .*

That's when he pulled away.

Nell's cry was more than a little indignant.

"Don't worry." She didn't have to see his face to know he was smirking. "I'll let you come before the night is out."

Before the night is out? It was six thirty, if that. How long was he going to keep her on edge like this?

But she knew for sure it would only take longer if she voiced her objection. Hoping for a point or two in her favor, she forced out a polite, "Thank you, Sir," instead.

Chuckling darkly, he ran fingertips slick with her own moisture down her sides. The wet trails cooled as he gripped her hips, making her shiver. "Don't think you can sweet talk me into letting you come sooner. You'll get your pleasure when and only when I choose to give it to you, understand?"

God-fucking-damn, she hadn't been this turned on in *years*. Not since early in her relationship with Micah—before he'd let her see the real him. But there was also a fear that hadn't existed twelve years ago.

She found herself pulling on the cuffs, checking them for possible weaknesses. It took every bit of self-control she had to be still again. *He's not Micah. Mistress Freya trusts him. He's not Micah.* "Yes, Sir." Her voice shook. She couldn't help it. "I understand."

"Good girl." He stepped away from her, leaving her feeling deserted and exposed. Her heart pounded so hard, she could feel her blood rushing through her veins, making her a little lightheaded.

Butterfly.

The word fluttered right there on the tip of her tongue. She wasn't fucking ready for this. Maybe she'd never be ready again.

But then the belt cracked against her skin, the sound so loud she jolted more from that than the pain. The initial burn dulled into a delicious throb after only a few seconds.

Tears sprang to her eyes—not because it hurt too much, but from sheer relief. It had been so fucking long since someone hurt her with her needs in mind instead of his, *and by God it felt good*.

The belt came down again, even harder this time, and her cry was one of ecstasy. This wasn't Micah. Everything felt different this time. All the scenes she loved between Jasper and Penny in Valhalla flashed through her mind. She could do this. She relaxed against the Saint Andrew's cross as she waited for the next stroke.

"That's my girl," Rafe murmured in her ear, his voice low and rough. Only then did the spanking begin properly.

He started up a steady rhythm, mere moments passing between each heavy impact. She could hear him exhale every time the leather bit her skin, and after a while, her breathing fell into sync with his.

Up and down the belt traveled in a careful path, from the top of her ass down to her tender sit spots, over and over and over. After a while, the burn stopped dulling. It built instead, until her ass felt like it was literally on fire, and she was sure every inch of the skin was bright red.

Without any warning, Rafe tossed the belt aside and plunged three fingers into her pussy, twisting them around, testing her wetness. Wrenching his fingers free, he leaned against her, his weight flattening her against the padded cross, and wrapped his wet fingers around her throat. "You liked that, didn't you, you little pain slut," he rasped into her ear. "I could spank you all night, and you'd just get wetter and wetter, until it dripped down your legs to the floor."

Nell swallowed, loving how it made his hand press even tighter against her windpipe. If only he'd squeeze harder, choke off her air for real, even if only for a few seconds.

As if reading her mind, Rafe's hand tightened around her throat. Her eyelids fluttered closed as she struggled to breathe, and she gave herself over to the different sensations coursing through her body.

The feel of his hand still tightening, his fingertips digging into the sides of her neck. The pulsing throb of her swollen, punished ass. The matching throb in her pussy that desperately longed to be filled. The burn of her lungs the longer she went without taking a real breath.

It was too much, all way too much, and not nearly enough at the same time. Not when his cock still wasn't buried deep inside her.

Her eyes flew open when at last Rafe released her throat. She drew in a ragged breath, and silvery-white dots danced before her eyes like tiny diamonds.

"Time to give your pussy what it wants, little girl." He notched his cock into her slit.

"Please!" She was about to start legit begging if he didn't fuck her right-the-fuck-now.

He rammed his hips forward, sliding all the way in with one hard stroke.

The sound that wrenched itself out of her throat was straight-up inhuman. How had she lived without this for over a year? Her body spasmed around his cock, clenching down on him, as if it was afraid of another thirteen-month drought.

"Your tight little pussy loves my cock, doesn't it?" Rafe said, pulling almost all the way out before slamming in again.

All the breath left her as he slammed her against the center of the cross. "Please, Sir," she gasped, her voice high and airy. "My pussy needs you so fucking bad. Fuck me as hard as you can. I'm begging you."

With a wordless growl of approval, he began pounding into her to the beat of the music, the slap of his hips against her ass in perfect time with the low, thundering bass. As the tempo intensified, so did he, fucking her so fast and hard, every muscle in her body tied up in knots.

Oh God, she was so close. If he pulled away now, denying her yet again, she would fucking die.

But it would seem that, unlike her last Dom, Rafe's sadism had its limits. Snaking an arm around her hip, Rafe found her clit with the pad of his middle finger. He rubbed in time with his thrusts, pushing exactly hard enough to send her flying over the edge.

Throwing her head back against his shoulder, Nell screamed so loudly it hurt her vocal cords. Her clenching pussy dragged him to completion seconds later. He bit the soft flesh where her neck met her shoulder as he shuddered behind her.

"So fucking good," Rafe muttered when at last they were both still. "Welcome back, kitten."

Nell kept as still as she possibly could, hardly even daring to breathe. As soon as she showered and dressed that morning, Rafe led her to a formal parlor, stripping her down to her lingerie and ordering her onto her hands and knees. Now he used her as a footstool while he drank coffee and tapped away at his laptop.

She was doing every single thing in her power to be perfect for him. No matter how the stiff threads of the old Persian rug dug into her bare knees and palms, or how much her back ached to bow beneath his boots.

Using her as furniture was one of the things Brian always refused to do, not understanding the kink himself, and generally only giving a shit about his own desires. It was Micah who first helped her experiment in forniphilia.

At first, it had been everything she dreamed of. Focusing one hundred percent of her mind and energy on a single, simple task—to stay as perfectly still as whatever inanimate object her Dom ordered her to become—was like her own personal form of meditation. And she was always wet as the Pacific by the time it was over.

But like all things with Micah, it only started out great. As time passed, and he grew more and more open with his cruelty, he began binding her into increasingly painful positions, far longer than was safe. If she dared complain, he'd gag and punish her, wielding a cane with enough force to draw blood.

Repressing a shudder, she closed her eyes and forced herself to focus on the moment. She was three thousand miles from L.A.—a whole-ass country away from Micah. And Rafe already checked in with her twice to make sure she was doing okay, even though she wasn't restrained.

Before she could fully get back into the right mindset, though, the clacking of keys came to an abrupt halt, and Rafe settled his boots on the floor. "Kneel here," he said, pointing beside his feet.

Nell scurried up into the required position, sitting back on her heels as she waited for further instruction. At first, Rafe didn't look at her. Instead, he continued lounging on the antique sofa, legs spread wide, the laptop balanced between his thighs. He took the final few sips of his coffee as his eyes moved from side to side, scanning the screen one more time.

With a satisfied nod, he put his empty mug on a side table and spun the computer around, plopping it down on the blue velvet cushion. "Take a look," he ordered.

She leaned forward, eyes widening as she took in the large, bold letters centered at the top of the page: Ways for Nell to Earn Orgasms.

"Um, yes please," she said, giving him a flirty look through her eyelashes.

One corner of his mouth quirked up. "Keep reading to the end and see if you still feel that way."

Intrigued, Nell looked down at the computer screen.

Ways for Nell to Earn Orgasms

Henceforth, Rafe Erikson (the Dominant) will withhold all orgasms from Nell Beaumont (the submissive), unless she completes one or more of the tasks necessary to earn them.

Each morning, the submissive will be given an opportunity to complete any of the tasks listed below. Each point earned will result in one orgasm provided by the Dominant (or a proxy of the Dominant) throughout the course of the day. A failure to complete any tasks will result in the submissive wearing a chastity device until the next morning.

The available tasks are as follows:

Make a list of people you wish were still in your life (1 use only)

- Email, call, or send a letter to one of the people on your list
- Do research toward figuring out your new dream job
- Make a list of required steps to make that dream a reality
- Work toward completing any of the steps on that list

If the submissive earns three or more points on a single day, she will be given an opportunity to choose one of her sexual fantasies. As a reward, the Dominant will do anything in his power to make that fantasy a reality.

The Dominant will ensure the submissive has at least as many orgasms as the number of points she earned on any given day.

Nell stared at the screen far longer than necessary, buying herself time. He couldn't possibly be serious, could he?

If she refused to go along with this ridiculous plan, though . . . a chastity device and zero orgasms? That would be the week from hell, not the perfect reintroduction to kink Mistress Freya had promised. She had to stop that from happening at all costs.

But there was no fucking way she could reach out to her family or old friends. She made her shitty choices, and now she had to live with the consequences. As if any of them would want to talk to her anyway.

Holly might.

The thought hit her like a baseball bat to the chest, making it impossible to breathe for several seconds. Closing her eyes, she focused on the tingling sensation in her fingertips—the one "normal" meditation technique she found that worked for her. As soon as she found her center again, she forced air slowly in and out of her lungs.

Okay, yes, Holly probably wanted to talk to her. They were Irish twins, born only days shy of a year apart, and were so alike in looks most people assumed they were actual twins. They couldn't have been more different in temperament, but that hadn't stopped them from being best friends for as long as either could remember. Holly and Nell had always been each other's ride or die . . . at least until Micah got into her head.

Nell would do anything to get back to that place with her older sister. But how in the actual hell could she earn back Holly's trust? She hadn't merely burned that bridge. She obliterated it.

"Why don't you say whatever's worrying you out loud," Rafe said, snapping her mind back into the present. He had that delightfully domineering look in his gray-green eyes again, but it softened when their gazes met. "Then we can work together to figure out if there's any way forward."

Nell opened her mouth with every intention of talking about her sister. But what came out instead was, "Will I seriously not get any more orgasms all week if I don't do any of this?" Apparently, her pussy had hijacked her brain—not shocking since it had been pulsing with need from the moment she read about Rafe's potential rewards.

The corners of Rafe's eyes crinkled the tiniest bit. It didn't look like he smiled or laughed very often. "As fun as that would be for me, no, this isn't mandatory. If you choose not to do it, we'll move on. Though I think a big part of you wants everything on this list to happen. I know how desperately you want to get back everything you lost. Whole new beautiful you, remember?"

Her fingertips traced the scars beneath her butterfly tattoo, the movement involuntary. She started cutting when she was seventeen, slicing the long, thin lines into her skin with a razorblade. She hadn't understood why she longed for the pain. Only that it eased an ache in her she lacked the knowledge or context to understand.

Holly found out eventually and made her promise never to do it again—a promise that became infinitely easier to keep when she stumbled into the BDSM lifestyle. Suddenly, the things she longed for had a proper name.

"And if you do these things . . ." The gentleness in Rafe's eyes turned to scorching heat. "Kitten, I can make every single one of your fantasies come true."

An involuntary shiver ran down her spine at the intensity in his eyes. God, he probably could make all her fantasies come true. She'd foolishly believed Micah could do it, and perhaps believing Rafe would make her an even bigger fool. And yet, there was something so fundamentally different about the man in front of her. If she held up her end, there was no doubt in her mind he'd hold up his.

And besides, what was the worst that could happen? Yeah, okay, maybe her family and friends would all reject her like she rejected them, and that would majorly suck. But if they didn't . . . if there was even the slightest chance of getting Holly and the others back in her life . . .

"All right," she said, hating how small and scared her voice sounded. "Let's do this, Sir."

His answering sigh sounded relieved more than anything else. As if he hadn't expected her to go along with it. "Good girl." Cupping her cheek, he leaned down to plant a hard kiss on her lips. "The laptop is yours. If you want any help, let me know. Otherwise, I'll let you be until you're ready to show me what you've done."

Relief flowed through her, loosening the ball of anxiety in her stomach. This would all be hard enough without someone breathing down her neck while she did it. "Thank you, Sir."

With a small nod, Rafe fished his phone out of his pocket and leaned back against the sofa's blue velvet upholstery. Nell waited until he was staring down at his phone before she returned her attention to the contract on the laptop screen.

Easiest task of all was making the list of people. She already knew who she wanted on it, even if she was too petrified to contact most of them. Opening up a blank document, she typed out the list that had been lurking around in her head for years.

People I Want Back in My Life

1. Holly (my sister)
2. Cady (my best friend from high school)
3. Ben (my other best friend from high school)
4. My mom
5. My dad

Her parents were the least likely to ever forgive her, and Nell couldn't blame them. Not after everything she put them through. But there was at least a chance with the others.

She left her old cell behind at Micah's when she ran away, so calling her sister was out of the question. And who knew where Holly lived these days, which meant a letter wouldn't work.

There was always a chance she still used the same email address, though. That would be easy enough to track down.

Double-clicking on Rafe's internet browser, she navigated to the login page for her old email address. Like the phone, she abandoned it when she left Micah. Though honestly, she hadn't looked at it much for years before that. Who would want to email her anyway?

Nell typed in the login info, but couldn't make herself hit enter. Her mind spun with all the ways this was a truly terrible idea.

It probably wouldn't even work. Nearly a decade had passed since she last emailed her sister. The chances she still used the same account were pretty slim. What if she'd gotten married? Presto chango, hello new email address.

Even if it *did* work, Holly would probably tell her to fuck off. Or, even worse, ignore her entirely.

And scariest of all, there could be emails from Micah in there. It would've been his only avenue to contact her or attempt to track her movements once he found her phone and credit cards on his nightstand.

She already earned a point by making the list. If she could get two more doing the job search thing, Rafe would still give her one of her fantasies today. It might be smart to take a day to consider the possible repercussions of this decision.

Fuck it.

Hitting the enter key with far more force than necessary, she held her breath as her inbox loaded.

Inbox 10,153

"Oh, good lord," she muttered under her breath.

Rafe glanced at her over the laptop screen. "Need help?"

Before she could answer, her gaze fell on the sender of an email she received at 12:53 that morning—Micah O'Neill.

He emailed her today? It would be exactly thirteen months since she left him later this week, the day before Halloween. Why in the actual fuck was he still emailing her?

She raked her gaze over the subject line and preview, unable to stop herself from reading the words.

More Progress – Noelle, I had another breakthrough in therapy yesterday and . . .

"Nell? I asked you a question."

Her gaze snapped up to meet his. "No, Sir. Thank you, but I've got this."

Right clicking on her ex's name, Nell chose *Find emails from Micah O'Neill*. Her eyes widened as she scrolled through the hundreds of unread emails, dating back to the day after she left. The oldest one was more what she had expected.

Where the fuck are you??? – How dare you leave, you little cunt! Get your ass . . .

In the beginning, he sent several emails of that ilk a day. But after a few months of that, he started sending only one a day, and from the looks of it, they got increasingly calmer and nicer.

Her heart pounded so fucking hard it was amazing Rafe didn't hear it. She could hear the rush of it in her ears, feel it in her skin. Part of her was desperate to know what all these emails contained, while the rest of her wanted nothing more than to throw the laptop across the room. Those two warring sides kept the cursor hovering over the email from that morning for over a minute.

Was he seriously in therapy? For her? The Micah she'd been with all those years thought he was the epitome of perfection. He never would've sought out any sort of help to better himself. Maybe her sudden departure was the wake-up call he needed.

She wouldn't ever go back to him, no matter how much therapy he got. Not after all the shit he did to her. But what if the emails could provide some sort of closure—help her move on?

Absolutely fucking not.

Before she could do something monumentally stupid, she clicked the little box to select every single email from Micah, and then hit the trash can icon. Relief flooded through her the second they were off her screen. It didn't matter what he had to say. Nothing would get her to take even a single step down that road again.

It took only a few seconds after that to find and copy Holly's email address, and she signed out of the account before anything else could tempt her. Nell smiled as she signed into her new account—the one she created on a library computer once she arrived in Tampa. She was *finally* learning, finally getting stronger. Micah wouldn't snare her in yet another of his endless traps.

Pulling up a new email, Nell loaded in Holly's email address, then typed *I left him, I love you, and I'm sorry* into the subject line. Hopefully that would be enough to get her to open the email instead of deleting it right off the bat.

Now for the hardest part. What could she possibly say that would convince Holly to speak to her again?

Okay, that was actually pretty obvious: the truth. As much of it as she could force herself to put down into words.

With a deep, steadying breath, she started typing.

Dear Holly,

The absolute most important thing I need you to know is that I'm sorry. I'm sorrier than I'll ever be able to say. Please give me a chance to prove to you how truly sorry I am for the things I said to you, the things I put you through.

I left Micah. It's been over a year, and I haven't seen him, spoken to him, nothing. He has no idea where I am or how to find me, and I'm keeping it that way. It wasn't long after the intervention that I started to realize everything you guys said was true. But by then, it was too late. I didn't know what to do, how to get out, where to go, anything at all. He had control over every single aspect of my life.

I was so scared and ashamed and confused and alone. I kinda checked out for a while. Went along with whatever I needed to do to survive. It wasn't until something bad enough happened that I finally snapped out of it and found my way out.

I'm safe now. I found kind people who I can trust, and they're helping me rebuild my life and learn how to be happy again. One of those people helped me find the courage to reach out to you.

If you never want anything to do with me again, I'll understand. I know how much I fucked up. That's why it took me this long to reach out to you. But if you can find it in your heart to at least consider the possibility of forgiving me, I want nothing more in the world than to talk to you.

Love,

Noelle

She read through the email a few times, making tiny tweaks until she was happy with it. Moving the cursor over the blue send button, she closed her eyes and forced her index finger to press down.

All the air rushed out of her lungs as soon as her finger lifted off the left click button. Holy fucking shit, she actually did it. She seriously let Rafe talk her into this shit. Into facing the guilt and burning humiliation of what she did all those years ago. And for what—orgasms? Was she really willing to torture herself for a sexual fantasy or two? Had she learned *nothing*?

What if Holly wrote back that she hated Nell and would never, ever forgive her? Maybe Holly moved on, and here she was, crashing through her sister's boundaries and hurting her even more.

Or what if the address was old, and Holly never saw it? Even if she did read it, that didn't mean she'd be willing to write back. Either way, Nell would be in the dark, having no idea which one it was, hating herself for ever daring to believe she could have Holly back.

Fucking hell, this was ridiculous. She used to be so happy. To look out at the world with unrestrained joy and hope. She hated the terrified, shrunken creature she'd become.

Before her mind could come up with even more doomsday scenarios, she opened a new tab and Googled the first career-related thing that popped into her head: *Jobs to help abused women*. Her racing mind calmed as soon as she hit enter. What if she could help other women escape situations like the one she left? Help them start over somewhere new and safe, the way Mistress Freya helped her? That would be fucking amazing.

Several of the search results were job sites, so she started scrolling through them, making a list in a new document of anything that sounded remotely interesting and bookmarking links for jobs that deserved a deeper dive.

Leaving her two lists, the latest job site, and her email to Holly open, she flipped the laptop around to face Rafe. "I've finished my tasks for today, Sir."

"Good girl," he said, setting his phone down next to his empty coffee mug and picking up the laptop. His eyes moved from side to side as he scanned each page, his blank expression giving nothing away. It wasn't until he finished reading through the final one that he arched his eyebrows. "Your parents named you Noelle and Holly?"

"We were both born right before Christmas, one year apart," she explained, one corner of her mouth twisting up into a wry smile.

"Which we realized when we were teenagers meant we were probably both conceived on their anniversary." She rolled her eyes, earning a tiny huff of a laugh from her stoic Dom.

"If you prefer Noelle, I can call you that instead. Your application only had—" He stopped speaking when she shook her head.

"I didn't start going by Nell until after I left Micah." Just saying his name sent anxiety twisting through her chest. "So I had to sign it like that so she'd know it was me. But I prefer Nell now, Sir."

Anytime Mistress Freya or one of the members at Valhalla said her actual name in their Dom/Domme voice, it had sent her into a full-blown panic spiral. It was the Mistress who realized she probably had one hell of a case of PTSD, and helped her pick a shortened version of her name that she truly loved.

"Understood," Rafe said, closing the laptop and setting it aside. "Now, by my count, you earned three points today. So why don't you come up here"—he patted his thigh, looking down at her with a wolfish smile—"and tell me one of your deepest, darkest fantasies."

CHAPTER 6
Rafe

"Ms. Beaumont, do you know why I told you to come to my office?" Rafe asked, leaning back in his desk chair and steepling his fingers.

Nell stood across the desk in a schoolgirl costume he found in a supply closet on the third floor, clasping and unclasping her hands in front of her stomach. "No, Professor Erikson, I don't." There was the hint of a tremor in her voice, and she wasn't quite meeting his eyes.

Fuck, she looked sexy in that skimpy little plaid skirt. It was clearly made for someone much shorter, and he couldn't stop staring at those ridiculously long, tan legs of hers. The blue and black butterfly wings of her tattoo were on full display.

Focus, damnit.

With a herculean effort, he dragged his gaze back up to her face. "I read your latest paper this morning." Pulling two stapled essays from the top left drawer, he set them on the desktop. "This is your paper." He pointed at the one on his right. "And this one was written last year by a student of my colleague Professor McLaren." He drummed his fingers on top of the essay to his left. "A student named Olivia Adams. Does that name ring any bells?"

Nell's eyes widened for a moment, before she wiped all traces of expression off her face. "No, Sir. I don't know her."

"Really," he drawled. "Then I'm curious to know how you turned in a paper identical to Olivia's."

Her mask slipped, revealing the panic in her eyes. "Sir, I—"

"Don't even try to make excuses," Rafe interrupted, the ring of command in his voice more than enough to shut her up. "Plagiarism is a *very* serious offence. Do you have any clue what's about to happen?"

Her lower lip trembled, and her eyes sparkled with actual tears. "Academic probation?"

"At the very least," Rafe said, steepling his fingers again.

Christ, this was fun. He almost never participated in scenes like this anymore, and frankly, he expected something less playful out of her. But she insisted she wanted to start with something that wasn't "scary." Since spooking her too badly would likely result in one or more broken bones—all of them his—that was perfectly fine with him.

Though he was fascinated to find out what her other fantasies entailed.

"Least?" she repeated. "What else—"

"It's at the dean's discretion whether he wishes to give you another chance or not. Considering you stole the entire paper, and not only a section of it, he may choose to expel you."

"No!" She lurched toward him, gripping the edge of the desk hard enough to turn her knuckles white. "Please, I can't be expelled. My parents would literally kill me."

Arching a single brow, Rafe said, "Perhaps you should've thought of that before you turned in someone else's work, Ms. Beaumont."

Nell blinked, sending a single tear down her cheek, where it caught on the corner of her mouth. Her tongue darted out, licking away the salty liquid, and if Rafe was hard before, that was nothing compared to now.

"Please, professor. I got overwhelmed, and I panicked, and I made a stupid decision. Stupidest decision I've ever made in my life. I know I shouldn't have done it, and I swear I'll never, ever do it again." She leaned forward, giving him an excellent view of her cleavage beneath her partially unbuttoned shirt. The little minx. "Please don't turn me in to the dean."

With a sigh, Rafe shook his head. "I'm afraid I can't do that. There's no way I can let this go unpunished. Not something this big."

"Punish me yourself, then," she begged, desperation in her voice, her face, her posture. "I'll write another paper—*two* more papers. Whatever you want. Or I can grade the weekly quizzes for you, or clean your office, or—"

Rafe held up a hand, silencing her. "Giving you extra work isn't enough. There has to be a real, genuine consequence, or I'm afraid the point won't be driven home." She started to speak, but he didn't give her the chance. "Enough. It's time to go see Dean Hale."

"*Please!*" she shouted, clasping her hands together in a pleading gesture. "I'll do anything, Professor. Anything at all to make this go away."

He started to stand, but settled back in his chair, regarding her with a thoughtful frown. "There's only one other thing I can think of that would make the proper impact," he said, doing his best not to smirk at the pun. "If you're willing to submit to a spanking, we can put this all behind us."

Nell's eyes were once again rounded with shock, and she opened her mouth several times before any sound came out. "A spanking?" she said in the faintest of whispers.

"Yes, Ms. Beaumont, a spanking. You've certainly earned it. Submit to my punishment, and I'll never say another word about this."

Her gulp was loud enough for him to hear across the desk. "How long of a spanking?"

He arched his brows again, staring into her beautiful brown eyes until she looked away, a blush reddening her cheeks. "As long as I think it needs to be for the lesson to take."

Nell straightened, her hands shaking as she smoothed out her white button-up, then adjusted her tie. Keeping her gaze firmly planted on the desk between them, she took a deep breath and forced out, "I agree to your terms, professor."

"I think that's a very wise decision," he said, keeping a stern look on his face by sheer force of will. "Now be a good girl and come over here."

Her gaze darted up to meet his for only a moment. "Over there, Sir?"

Rolling his chair away from the desk, he patted his thigh twice. "If you want this all to go away, Ms. Beaumont, I expect you to be over my knee in the next thirty seconds."

A shiver ran through her, and she chewed on her bottom lip. "Isn't there any other—"

"Place yourself over my knee or go upstairs to Dean Hale's office. The choice is yours." Her whimper made him want to bend her over that desk and fuck her senseless. With what was, frankly, the patience of a saint, he stayed perfectly still, counting down the seconds in his head. As they neared the deadline, he said aloud, "Five, four, three . . ."

She scrambled around the desk at last, practically launching herself across his lap in her panic. Rafe took firm hold of her hips as she very nearly toppled over onto the floor, pulling her back up into the position he wanted.

"Now," Rafe said, letting one heavy hand rest upon her upturned bottom, "I expect you to take your spanking like a good girl. You know you've earned this. Don't make things any harder on yourself than they already are."

There was that whimper again that made his cock throb with the need to be inside her. Mouth, pussy, ass—he didn't care, so long as it was tight and wet and *hers*.

"Let's begin." Raising his hand, he brought it down twice, once for each cheek.

With a long, low wail, Nell squirmed over his thighs, reaching back with one hand, whether to rub at the sting or protect herself from further punishment he didn't know. Nor did he care. Taking firm hold of her wrist with his free hand, he pinned her arm against her back.

"Sir, please, it hurts." She squirmed again, only stopping when he twisted her arm back enough to make her cry out.

"Please do remember this is a punishment." His voice dripped with sarcasm. "It's *supposed* to hurt."

She sniffed a few times, but finally relaxed her muscles, the fight going out of her like a candleflame caught in a gust of wind. "Yes, Sir," she mumbled.

"Good. Now be still." He covered her ass and the tops of her thighs with several more hard spanks, using most of his considerable strength. Holding back wouldn't be doing her any favors.

Crying out at the most severe of the impacts, Nell kicked and squirmed. If he didn't have such a strong hold on her arm, she would've wriggled right off his lap.

"Enough," Rafe said, using the sternest Dom voice in his repertoire.

She went still as a statue.

"I told you to be still. If you can't listen on your own, I'm going to have to give you some incentive."

She started to ask what he meant, but he flipped her skirt up before she got more than a single word out. Nell gasped, her ass cheeks clenching together beneath her white cotton panties. "Naughty girls who won't accept their punishments get spanked on their bare bottoms," Rafe said, running a fingertip beneath the elastic waistband. "Is that really what you want? Or are you ready to be good and . . ." He let the rest of his sentence trail off.

After the silence dragged on for several seconds, she craned her neck around, trying to look at his face. "Sir?" For the first time, she sounded genuinely scared.

Letting his hand trail down the crack of her ass, he cupped her pussy, squeezing hard enough to make her flinch. "What is this, Ms. Beaumont? Is this a wet spot on your panties? Are you *enjoying* your punishment?"

She let the curtain of her long hair block her face from his view. "I don't know what you—"

"Don't lie to me." It came out as a growl. "I'm only going to give you one more chance to tell the truth, and you do *not* want to find out what happens if you lie again. Are you enjoying your punishment?"

Nell squeezed her legs together, trapping his hand between her thighs like a vice. Fucking hell, she was strong. It made her submission exponentially sexier to him. After several more long seconds, she whispered, "Yes, Sir."

"So all the crying and flailing . . ." He slipped a finger beneath her panties and slid it into her tight, wet pussy, making her moan. "Nothing but an act?" His tone practically dared her to answer in the affirmative and see what happened.

With a great, shuddering breath, she forced out another soft, "Yes, Sir."

"Oh, Nell." He added a second finger, curling them until her whole body spasmed. "You have no idea how much worse this just got for you." Gripping her around the waist, he hauled her up to stand in front of him. With firm hands on her hips, he positioned her exactly as he wanted her, standing between his spread thighs, facing the desk. "Hand me your tie."

Nell's shoulders tensed at the command, but she didn't hesitate. Slipping her tie off with trembling fingers, she held it behind her back for him. His hand brushed against hers as he took the red, plaid silk, making her jump.

"Good girl. Now the shirt."

Her head whipped around so fast, her neck cracked. "Sir?"

For the first time, he allowed some of his lust to show in his eyes. Her breath hitched at the sight of it. "Naughty little girls who enjoy their spankings need more severe punishments. Do as you're told."

Nell's eyelids fluttered closed as she faced forward again, her breaths heavy and fast as she fumbled over the row of tiny buttons. It took over a minute for her to undo them all. When she finally pulled her shirttails free of the pleated skirt and let the sleeves slide slowly down her arms, her pale back was bare beneath.

Rafe took the shirt with one hand, and slipped her long, wavy hair over her shoulder with the other. "Did you come to my office without a bra on purpose?" He traced a single fingertip down her spine. "You're nothing but a little slut, aren't you?"

She shuddered as goosebumps popped up all over her skin, but didn't say a word.

Giving her bottom a single, firm swat, he said, "Answer me."

"Yes, Sir." Her voice shook with lust instead of fear.

Reaching around, he grabbed her nipples, squeezing them hard enough to make her throw back her head and moan. "Yes, what?"

"Yes, I did it on purpose, Sir. I *am* a slut." The words came out in a breathy rush.

"Was that your plan all along? To get yourself out of trouble by seducing me?"

As he pinched and rolled and pulled, she arched her back, practically shoving her luscious ass in his face. She panted as she gasped out, "Nothing else I did got you to fuck me."

They both stilled at the confession. The worry in her eyes when she looked over her shoulder made it abundantly clear she hadn't meant to say that out loud.

Gripping her chin, he stood, putting them nose to nose. "You want me to fuck you, you little slut?" The malice in his eyes made the breath catch in her throat. "Be careful what you wish for."

Rafe released her as he dropped down into his chair. Snatching up her tie from where it fell, he wrenched her arms behind her back with enough force to make her yelp. The strip of plaid silk wasn't nearly long enough for a proper double-column tie, so he had to improvise, twisting the fabric into a double-knotted bow one would use to tie a child's sneakers.

Standing, he wrapped her hair once around his fist, using it to guide her around to the other side of the desk. After sweeping the papers off the desktop, he pressed the same hand between her shoulder blades as the essays fluttered noisily to the floor. Not that he had to press hard; she went willingly, bending at the waist until her torso lay flat against the polished wood. Fucking hell, he loved the way her breasts pressed outward as they flattened, and how her long legs forced her ass up into the air.

He gave her hair a final sharp tug, making her suck in air through her teeth, before relinquishing his hold. Running his hands down her bare sides, he gripped her hips over her skirt, his thumbs toying at the crack of her ass. "I think it's high time you were bared to me, don't you?"

Nell moaned in response, shutting her eyes tight and pressing her left cheek against the desktop. "Yes, Sir."

Grinning, he flipped her skirt up again, securing it beneath her bound hands. The white cotton panties beneath were so sweet—so incredibly innocent.

Not at all appropriate for this naughty little slut.

Gripping them in one fist, he squeezed them up between her cheeks, dragging the fabric roughly across her pussy and clit. Nell pressed her legs together with a low moan, but he shoved his knee between her thighs, forcing them back apart. "If you can't stay open for me on your own, I'll tie your legs to the desk. Do I make myself clear?"

Her ass clenched at his words, but she kept her legs spread wide. "Yes, professor."

"Good girl." Slipping his fingers beneath the waistband of her panties, he yanked them down to mid-thigh, where her spread legs kept them firmly in place. He traced a soft line across the backs of her thighs, just above the elastic. "If these fall down, I'll know you disobeyed me, and your punishment will only get worse."

Her legs snapped out even wider, as far as the stretchy fabric would allow. Rafe couldn't help but grin at her instinctive reaction—and he fucking loved the improved view.

He brushed his thumb over her clit, his touch so light he wasn't even sure she'd feel it. But she was so keyed up, her whole body jerked as if he used a vibrator on its highest setting. Pushing her hips back, she tried to chase his hand, but he pulled away. "Patience, Ms. Beaumont."

Her moan was somewhere between lust and despair. "You said I could come three times." She was practically crying. "If I did three tasks, I got three orgasms."

"That I did," he said, removing his cufflinks, rolling his sleeves up one at a time. "But I never said *when*. We have all day, little girl." He kept his gaze on her as he made a slow circle around the desk, taking in the contrast of her skin—smooth and tan across so much of her gorgeous body, but scarred and pale in the places she usually kept hidden. It meant the fucking world to him that she bared those places to his eyes.

He wanted to follow each and every one of the lines on her back, ass, and thighs with a fingertip. Trace the partial name engraved onto her hip. Follow the path of pain that made her the amazing woman bent over the desk before him—that brought her to him.

He hated that she went through such horrific things, and would beat Micah to a bloody pulp if ever he got the chance. But those scars were part of her now, and he wasn't afraid of them. He wanted every single part of her he could get.

As he passed by the front of the desk, he opened the largest drawer, pulling out a long, thick wooden paddle. There wasn't a more perfect implement for an academic scene like this.

"Now," he said, gripping the handle with its smooth, rounded end. He gave a couple of practice swings into his palm, enjoying the way the sound made her jump. "Since the spanking ended up being so enjoyable for you, let's see if something a little more severe gets my point across."

Nell started to say, "Sir, I—" in a pleading sort of voice. But he swung the paddle down without warning, and the impact drove all the air from her lungs. She didn't even breathe as the next two swings of the paddle came down across the center of her ass.

It wasn't until after stroke number four that she finally gasped air back into her lungs, using it to let out a sharp cry. Three more and tears flooded her eyes.

Fuck, her tears were beautiful.

Pain slut or no, a severe wooden paddle like the one he wielded hurt like a motherfucker. If she was anything like the other subs he scened with who got off on pain, the tears would make her burn even hotter.

Sure enough, when he took a short break to plunge two fingers into her pussy, she was dripping wet.

A new need coursed through him, so strong he felt the twist of desperation in his chest. He had to see how much of his pain she could take.

Without a word of warning, he started up again, letting the paddle travel up and down to reach every part of her ass. The tears escaped her eyes by the time he brought the paddle down on her sit spots five times in a row. By the final stroke, she pressed her forehead against the surface of the desk, her whole body shaking with sobs.

"Beautiful," he said, running the paddle's lacquered wood over her red, swollen flesh. It only made her cry harder. If his cock wasn't inside her soon, he would fucking explode.

Before he could act on that impulse, the door behind him flew open, hard enough to crash against the adjacent wall. "Good God, Erikson, what on earth is all that racket? Some of us are trying to grade papers, you know."

Ah, it was time for the next stage of Nell's naughty little fantasy. Perfect.

Rafe knew his bulk hid most of Nell from Camden's view. Letting the paddle fall to his side, he turned to face the new player in their scene —and very nearly fucked it all up by laughing.

Apparently, Camden decided a suit was too boring for a professorial look, and had instead gone with gray slacks, a white tee, and—honest to God—a blue and gray cardigan. It looked absurd on his huge, muscular frame. The black-framed hipster glasses definitely didn't help matters.

Luckily, Camden covered for Rafe's fumble. He smirked as he said, "Oh. Who do you have there?"

"Nell Beaumont." Realizing she'd fallen silent, he glanced down, taking in the tenseness of each muscle, and the new alertness in her eyes. She was clearly listening to every word.

Bright blue eyes sparkling with mischief, Camden stepped the rest of the way into the room, closing the door behind him. "I've gotten enough sass from Beaumont to last me a lifetime. It's about time someone did something about it."

Rafe let his empty hand fall onto Nell's punished flesh, squeezing until she cried out again. "You've been giving Professor Reid trouble, as well?" It was more demand than question.

Her eyes narrowed. If she was a cat, her hackles would be raised. "I didn't cheat in his class, if that's what you mean."

"I don't care for your tone, young lady," Rafe said, plunging three fingers into her pussy, pressing his thumb against the tight ring of her asshole. Without any lubrication, he could only get his finger in up to the first knuckle, but that was enough. He pinched his fingers together until she cried out, then took a fistful of her hair with his other hand. Shoving her forward, he rammed her thighs against the desk with bruising force, stretching out her torso and neck until her chin hung over the far edge. "Care to join me?"

Camden's answering grin made him look like a cross between a drunk frat boy and an excited puppy. It took everything in him not to roll his eyes. Rafe knew a lot of their guests loved the whole cheerful fuckboy persona, but he sure as fuck didn't get the appeal. If her next fantasy involved additional men, he'd be talking to the more serious Doms in residence, Mason or Jonathan.

Not seeming to notice Rafe's annoyance, Camden made his way around the desk, his gaze raking over Nell's nearly naked form. He stopped directly in front of her face, the bulge of his erection only inches from her mouth.

"I've been wanting to teach this smart mouth a lesson all year," he said, brushing his thumb over the seam of her lips. "Open up, baby."

She obeyed without hesitation, closing her eyes and stretching her mouth as wide as she could in the awkward position. As Camden undid the front of his slacks, Rafe got back to work with the paddle, wanting her ass to be a true, deep crimson before he fucked it.

It wasn't long before the timbre of her cries changed dramatically, and he glanced up to find Camden already balls deep in her mouth. Jesus, did she even have a gag reflex? He froze, watching for several seconds as the other Dom face-fucked his sub, the man's enormous cock repeatedly disappearing into her throat with apparent ease.

Fuck it, her ass was crimson enough.

Leaning into her, his own trapped erection grinding against her dripping pussy, Rafe reached across the desk, sliding open the top right drawer. Inside, right where he left it, was a small bottle of lube.

"I know you want me to fuck your tight little pussy," he growled in her ear. "But bad little girls like you have to take it in the ass."

Her whole body spasmed beneath him, and for a moment, he thought she was panicking. He straightened at once, watching her bound hands for the signal they agreed on if she was unable to speak her safeword. But her hands stayed exactly as they were, clasped together at the small of her back.

Rafe's lips curled into a slow, wolfish grin. "Let's get you ready for me, naughty girl." Cracking open the bottle of lube, he spread her cheeks wide, squeezing a long ribbon directly onto her asshole. She tried to clench her ass together the second the cold, clear liquid hit her, but his hand forced her to remain open to him.

Without any warning, he plunged one finger in, pushing past the tight ring even as her body instinctively tried to force him out. "You better relax," he said, adding a second finger, attempting to stretch them apart. "I'm fucking you either way. It'll be a lot easier for you if you don't fight me."

Nell made a long, low humming noise in her throat, which very nearly sent Camden over the edge. "*Fuck*," he half-shouted, pulling out until only the tip was still in her mouth. His grip on the sides of her face tightened. "Don't do that again until I tell you to, understood?"

The impish look in her eyes made Rafe want to spank her and fuck her and absolutely fucking cherish her all at once. How she could still be so naughty, so playful after all she'd been through was quite beyond him. The woman was a goddamn marvel.

After several seconds, she managed a very garbled, "Yes, Sir."

Repressing a chuckle, Rafe withdrew his fingers and grabbed the paddle again. "Maybe this will loosen you up." The dark promise in his voice made Nell's shoulders tense. But Camden was hard at work on her throat again, making it impossible for her to see what he was up to.

Covering the long, straight handle of the paddle with copious amounts of lube, he then pressed the rounded tip against her rear hole. She stiffened, one of her legs actually kicking out as if to knock him away.

With his free hand, Rafe gave her three harsh smacks on her right ass cheek. "Be still."

Nell settled down immediately, calmed by the command in his voice. And as he pumped the paddle handle in and out of her, its squared edges undoubtedly uncomfortable as fuck, she finally relaxed.

"Good girl." Tossing the paddle aside, he opened the front of his slacks, groaning as his cock sprang free. He'd denied himself for long enough.

It took mere seconds to apply a healthy dose of lube, and then he was finally, miraculously pressing into her. Christ almighty, she felt good. "So . . . fucking . . . tight," he gasped out, pushing, pushing, refusing to withdraw until he buried himself inside her.

When at last his hips pressed against the deep red of her punished ass, he took a moment to collect himself. The last thing he wanted was to come quickly and ruin the scene, but fucking hell, it felt like his cock was in a vise.

"You'd better get moving," Camden said, voice strained. He had his eyes shut tight, and beads of sweat dotted his forehead. "I'm not sure how much longer I can last." Apparently he hadn't expected her to be quite so adept at deep-throating either.

Nell's fantasy was quite clear about being fucked by two professors at once. He'd stalled for long enough.

Gripping her hips with bruising pressure, Rafe pulled out most of the way before slamming back in. She made that humming noise again, cutting it off abruptly when Camden lightly slapped her face.

He allowed himself two more slow withdrawals, followed by hard, fast thrusts. Just to get them both used to the feeling. And then all bets were off.

Rafe drove into her with a speed and violence that surprised even him. The dirty little slut deserved it. Cheating on purpose to get his attention, lying to seduce him, swallowing another man's cock when she was supposed to be worshipping his, only his. She belonged to *him*.

He lost himself so utterly in the fantasy, he jumped when Camden said, "Hold her up for me."

It took him a moment to realize what Camden meant. Then with a hard grin, he wrapped her long hair around his fist once, twice. The other Dom pulled out of her mouth at the last second, and Nell screamed as Rafe hauled her up.

Wrapping a giant hand around his own cock, Camden pumped furiously. Rafe continued fucking her, his movement making her torso rock back and forth in time with his thrusts. Not seeming to mind the moving target, Camden let loose a string of profanity as he finally came, shooting thick jets of come onto her chest, neck, and chin.

With a roar, Rafe pulled out completely, yanking her all the way up by her hair. A few quick pulls, and the tie fell away from her hands. Before she could even react to her new freedom, he spun her around, pushing her down onto the desk on her back.

"Hold her arms above her head," he ordered, ripping off her panties and tossing them aside. He flipped her legs up over his shoulders as Camden pressed her wrists against the desktop with one hand.

There was barely any resistance as Rafe plunged back into her ass.

Nell threw back her head and screamed, her legs clenching around his neck, cutting off some of his air.

"Put your other hand around her throat." He had to force the words out between clenched teeth. "Show her who's in fucking control."

As Camden followed his lead without question, Rafe wrapped an arm around one of her muscular thighs. His thumb found her clit again, but this time, he had no intention of teasing her. Her hips bucked as he pressed hard against the tiny bundle of nerves, then began a circular motion in perfect rhythm with his thrusts.

The skirt bunched up around her waist, her panting breaths, the way her face screwed up in mingled pain and ecstasy, her come-covered breasts bouncing each time his pelvis slapped against her skin—

"Fucking hell!" He was going to lose control any fucking second.

He pinched her clit hard enough to make her scream again. And then they were both coming together, her ass spasming around him as his whole body jerked, no trace of rhythm left.

When at last they both stilled, Rafe lowered her legs to his sides and pulled her up into his arms. He didn't even spare a single thought for the mess it made of his clothes to press her chest against his, splaying his hands across her back. All he knew was that he wanted to touch as much of her bare skin as possible.

Face buried in his neck, there was something very like awe in her voice when she whispered, "Thank you."

CHAPTER 7
Nell

The glowing green numbers on the bedside clock read 3:08. Grabbing the pillow from beneath her head, Nell pressed it tight as she could against her face and screamed as loudly as she dared. God only knew what would happen if she woke the man sleeping beside her.

After the day she had, trouble sleeping should've been impossible. She'd been fucked, spanked, licked, and bound. Massaged, bathed, fed, and fucked some more. Every inch of her body hurt in the most delicious, languid way.

Never in her life had someone accessed all her body's secrets so expertly. Like a master musician picking up a dusty instrument and making it truly sing.

No, after all that, she should be sleeping like a fucking baby. Yet she'd spent hours staring at the fireplace, watching the fire die down until the room plunged into near-total darkness. And here she was after three in the morning, tossing and turning and screaming into a feather pillow.

Propping herself up on one elbow, she gazed across the bed, finding the small rectangular shadow on Rafe's nightstand. He let her check her email on his phone twice that evening—once before dinner and again right before bed. Both times, her heart raced as she signed in, a nause-ating mixture of hope and anxiety whirling around in her gut. And both times, she plummeted into misery when the inbox loaded without a response from Holly.

But that was *hours* ago. And Holly lived on the west coast; it was barely after midnight in Seattle.

Waking her new Dom to check her email was obviously out of the question. If she didn't have to wake him, though . . .

Nell climbed out of bed with such slowness and care, she suspected a glass of water set on the other side of the mattress wouldn't even ripple. Watching Rafe's dark form beneath the duvet, she tiptoed around the foot of the bed, stopping every time he so much as twitched. It felt like an eternity before she made it to his nightstand, though it probably took under a minute.

Using only her fingertips, she lifted the phone from the nightstand with painstaking care, ensuring the charger didn't so much as brush against the wood.

Just as she unplugged his phone, he let out a single, loud snore. The charging cable tumbled from her fingers when she jumped, clacking against the nightstand on its way to the floor. There wasn't anything she could do about it, as both hands were occupied with juggling the phone she almost dropped at the same time.

By the time she pressed the phone securely against her chest, her heartbeat raced so fucking fast, she feared she might have a literal heart attack. But Rafe's eyes remained closed, and he returned to his slow, gentle breathing after a couple of seconds.

Jesus, that was close. She needed to get to the safety of the en suite bathroom before anything else could go wrong.

Creeping like a thief in the night (which she technically was), she made her way toward the bathroom as silently as possible. A soft blue light emanated from the crack in the door, guiding her footsteps across the room like a beacon. She didn't remember a nightlight in any of the plugs, but clearly she hadn't paid close enough attention.

Shit, did the door have squeaky hinges? She couldn't remember.

Holding her breath, she eased it open without a sound. Relief flowing through her, she hurried inside, the tiles toasty beneath her bare feet. A place as fancy as Fairford Manor apparently required heated floors.

Taking her time, she pushed the door closed as slowly as she could, not daring to make a single additional sound. Satisfied, she turned around—and nearly blew everything by laughing.

The fucking *toilet* was glowing.

Good God, could this place get any fancier? She noticed the bidet when she used the facilities before bed—hard not to given the heated seat and large remote—though she'd been too nervous to use it. But apparently the thing even had a light sensor, because it definitely wasn't glowing before.

Shaking her head at the ridiculousness of it all, she shuffled over to the toilet, taking a seat. If Rafe came looking for her, she could simply claim she needed to pee.

The blue light disappeared as she pressed her thighs together, plunging the room into total darkness. Resting her hands on her lap, she tapped his phone screen with one thumb. His wallpaper was a picture of the Manor at the height of summer, its front gardens a riot of colorful plants and flowers.

With guilt forming a ball in the pit of her stomach, she entered his password, consoling herself with the fact she didn't memorize it on purpose. She had no choice but to learn how to be sneaky in her years under Micah's thumb, and now it was second nature.

Pulling up his internet browser, she found the tab with her email and signed in. Hope surged in her chest as the inbox loaded, only to die seconds later.

There was no sign of Holly's name.

As worst-case scenarios started boiling over in her head, she forced herself to close her eyes and take several deep, calming breaths. They hadn't spoken in almost a decade. Of course Holly might need time to process before she emailed back. Hell, if this was an old email she hardly ever checked, she might not have even seen it. There was no reason to freak out.

Yet.

Still very much freaking out, she made sure the phone looked exactly like when she opened it, then started to stand. But something kept her rooted to the heated toilet seat with Rafe's phone still glowing in her hand.

Don't fucking do it, warned a livid voice in her head. A voice that sounded very much like Holly the last time they were together.

Nell frowned down at the phone as she pulled up the internet browser again. Ever since that morning, a single word ricocheted around in the back of her mind—closure.

She wouldn't respond to Micah. She legit never wanted to see or speak to him again, zero exceptions. But maybe, just maybe, if she read his words—learned about everything he'd done to try to make up for the years of abuse, and got an actual, genuine apology . . .

Maybe it would help her finally move on for good. Stop looking over her shoulder every damn second of the day.

With Holly's voice berating her in her head, she signed out of her new email and into her old one.

Immediately, her gaze zeroed in on his name. His latest email arrived like clockwork at 12:48 that morning. She went to open it, but stopped dead when she saw the subject line: *I see you found all my emails at last.*

Well, fuck. She should've known Micah would have her password. He'd needed total control over every aspect of her life.

The phone app showed more of a preview than Rafe's laptop, and she found her gaze hungrily flying over the additional words.

Dearest Noelle, I can't tell you what a relief it is to know you're safe. I've worried each and every m . . .

Holding her breath, she tapped on the email, feeling like a hand gripped her heart, twisting and tearing it without reserve.

Dearest Noelle,

I can't tell you what a relief it is to know you're safe. I've worried each and every moment since the day you disappeared. At first, part of me was afraid you hadn't left of your own free will. That you had been taken from me.

But then, with time, I realized that of course you left. How could you not with the way I treated you? Here I was, with the most precious thing in all the world in my possession, and I acted not only like a fucking fool, but like a monster.

I should have revered you. Cherished each and every occurrence of your submission. Rewarded you beyond measuring for your trust and your love. Instead, I did what so many fools do when they gain power over another. I tried to break you, just to prove to myself that I could.

I did so many things that go beyond the possibility of forgiveness. I'm not writing this to try to get you back. The last several months of intensive therapy have made it so very clear to me that whatever trust you once put in me has been irrevocably broken.

I needed you to know how very sorry I am, and that you don't need to worry about this happening again to another girl. I may never again trust myself with a submissive, but if I do, it'll be after months of more therapy, if not years. I won't risk hurting another the way I hurt you, even if that means I spend the rest of my life alone.

I hope you find peace and happiness in your life. You deserve it.

Love,

Micah

Nell stared at the screen for a long time after she finished, her eyes no longer focusing. The Micah she knew would never have been able to say the things she just read. Hell, he probably wouldn't have even been able to think them.

Was it possible thirteen months of soul searching and therapy could really have such a profound effect on a person?

Or was it much more likely he realized berating and insulting her would never win her back. But manipulation and pretty words actually stood a chance.

Well, at least Micah was right about one thing in his email—her trust in him was definitely irrevocably broken.

Signing out before she could do anything else stupid, she once again got all the tabs looking exactly like when Rafe put his phone down for the night. Now all she had to do was put it back without him waking up.

Figuring she might as well actually use the facilities before she went back to bed, she set his phone on the edge of the counter.

Every muscle in her body tensed as the phone crashed to the floor. *Fuck, fuck, fuck!* After being so careful this whole time, one stupid moment of inattention—

"Nell?" Rafe's low voice carried through the door, hoarse and groggy with sleep.

She froze, listening, hoping he only partially awakened. That he fell back asleep without noticing she was gone.

"Nell, are you all right?" His voice was already halfway across the suite. "I thought I heard something fall."

With no more time to waste, she swooped down, groping around for the phone in the dark. Fucking fuck, where was it? Any second, Rafe would walk through that door, flick on the light, and find her naked on the toilet, trying to find his phone in the dark. She didn't even want to guess what he'd do for such a transgression. If only she could fucking *see.*

Inspiration hit her like a bolt of lightning. She knew exactly where she could get the light she needed.

Nell spread her legs wide, and blue light came pouring out of her nether regions.

Before she could stop herself, she let out a single bark of surprised laughter. Clamping a hand over her mouth, she smothered the way-too-loud sound, but it was too late.

Rafe called out, "What's going on in there?" from the other side of the door. It was impossible to tell if he sounded amused or suspicious.

Blood pounding through her veins like the rush of a tidal wave, she snatched the phone up from the tile floor and, without any other options available, threw it in the trash can, covering it with a few dirty tissues. She only just straightened up when Rafe partially opened the door, poking his head in. He must've turned on the floor lamp in the sitting area on his way by, because a dim light fell across half his face.

"Are you okay in here?" Oh yeah, he definitely suspected something. It was written all over his face.

Folding her hands primly over her lady bits, she gave him a sheepish smile. "I needed to use the bathroom, but I accidentally shut the door too hard. I didn't mean to wake you."

His lips flattened into a straight line, and he pushed the door the rest of the way open, leaning against the frame with his arms crossed over his stomach.

Shit, shit, *shit*, he was going to figure it out. Would he merely punish her for something like this, or would he kick her out of the Manor entirely?

Oh, she was so fucked. She tried to remember where she put Dale the Lexus Driver's business card.

"I also heard you laugh," Rafe said, a sense of challenge in his voice. "Care to tell me what you found so funny as you sat here alone in the dark?"

"Oh, that was because of this." She spread her legs wide again, releasing the blue glow. "Look! I have a magic vajayjay!"

Eyebrows shooting up, he looked down at her spread thighs, blinking and shaking his head slightly, like the gif that was so popular for a while. She was starting to worry he thought she said something monumentally stupid when he burst out laughing.

Seconds later, she joined him. She hadn't gotten to laugh properly at the thought the first time.

"All right, you ridiculous thing. Finish up, then come out here so I can examine this magical *vajayjay* of yours." Still chuckling, he went out into the suite, shutting the bathroom door behind him.

Sweet baby Jesus that was close. And it wasn't like she was out of the woods yet. After they were done with whatever he planned to do with her vagina, there was a better than average chance he'd notice his phone was missing.

Unless she managed to completely wear him to exhaustion. Her lips lifted up at one corner. That wasn't the worst plan she ever had. She'd just have to live with being tired as fuck tomorrow.

Hopefully Rafe would share his coffee.

CHAPTER 8
Rafe

He was exhausted the next morning, and clearly Nell was doubly so. The poor thing looked like she barely slept a wink all night—not surprising given everything that happened the day before.

Their three AM fuckfest probably didn't help matters. Jesus, she liked it hard. No matter how he pounded into her, she always seemed to need more. It left him utterly in her thrall. How any man could hurt this intoxicating creature instead of worshipping her was quite beyond his understanding.

Rafe could tell she was trying to be his perfect little footstool again, on her hands and knees in the blood-red bustier and matching lace panties she'd chosen that morning. But her chin kept falling toward her chest, and her back started to bow in the middle. She needed some caffeine or a nap stat.

"Okay, little girl," he said, moving his feet to the floor. "Kneel up for me now."

Her movements were slow and clumsy—a far cry from the lithe grace he was used to. "Here," he said, holding out his half-empty coffee mug. "You look like you need this more than I do."

She looked at him like he just offered her diamonds and riches. "Oh, *thank* you," she said, grabbing the mug and downing the rest of its contents in three large gulps. When she came up for air, she grimaced, though she tried to hide it.

Smirking, Rafe asked, "Not used to black coffee?"

"I'm more of a tea drinker." She wore the most adorable little self-conscious smile. Like she was embarrassed of her caffeinated drink preferences but didn't mind him knowing that. "When I do drink coffee, though, you can bet I load it up with cream and sugar."

Rafe rolled his eyes. "If you can't even taste the coffee anymore, what's the point?"

She laughed, a hint of a blush on her cheeks. "That *is* the point. If I actually liked coffee, I wouldn't have to hide the flavor with better tasting things."

"I'll keep that in mind." The small, amused smile felt so foreign on his face. He saw it on others plenty, but hardly ever felt a need to smile himself. What was this woman doing to him?

Needing to get back into familiar territory, Rafe spun the laptop around, pushing it in front of her. "You get to work while I go see about rectifying our current lack of caffeine."

"Yes, Sir." She started clicking away before he even stood. When he glanced back from the parlor door, she was frantically typing, hitting the keys with enough force that he winced. The laptop was brand fucking new.

Not that he could bring himself to scold her. He headed for the kitchen without so much as a single word. It couldn't be more abundantly obvious her anxiety was going haywire while she waited for a response from her sister. For fuck's sake, she even went so far as to steal his phone, her desperation to check her email in the middle of the night making her forget he had a password. At least he assumed she forgot. Nothing on his phone looked out of place when he checked this morning, but maybe he should change his password anyway, just in case.

He would've punished her if the whole thing wasn't so fucking heartbreaking. Well, and then she made the joke about the bidet light. He couldn't have stopped himself from laughing if he tried. (And he did try, exceptionally hard.) How the hell could he spank her after that?

So he fucked her instead, wearing both of them out to the point of total exhaustion. Afterward, he only stayed awake long enough to make sure she finally fell asleep—though he pretended to be out cold so she could retrieve his phone from the bathroom. Chivalry isn't dead.

What was it about this woman that made him want to break all his own rules?

Rafe nodded at Mason and his current sub—a pretty, petite blonde he'd never seen at the Manor before—as he passed through the dining room. The Belgian waffle smothered in mixed berries and whipped cream on the plate in front of them made his mouth water. He and Nell would definitely have to make some time for a proper breakfast after she finished her morning tasks. He could practically taste the Vermont maple syrup.

Only problem was, they'd never make it to breakfast on half a mug of coffee apiece.

The kitchen door swung back and forth on its two-way hinges after he pushed his way through. "Gabriel—"

"Back so soon?" the head chef interrupted, glancing up from his stand mixer. From the looks of it, he'd been adding vanilla to a new batch of whipped cream. "Luca, get him another cup of coffee." The newest member of Gabriel's daytime kitchen staff moved off toward the ridiculously fancy coffeemaker. Rafe had been forbidden from ever touching the thing, with all its knobs and buttons.

"Actually, can I also get some tea?" Rafe said, stopping Luca in his tracks. "I'm not sure what she prefers, so do you mind making up a tray with a few options? I want to make sure there's at least one thing she likes."

Every head in the kitchen turned his way by the time he stopped speaking. They stared at him as if he'd delivered his request in song and dance.

Rafe drew his brows together, glowering at them. "What?"

Gabriel's two underlings found their work all-engrossing all of a sudden. For his part, Luca hit far more buttons on that ridiculous contraption than necessary to make a mug of black coffee.

The head chef himself watched Rafe with pursed lips that did little to hide his smile. Rafe's glower didn't seem to have any effect on him.

"You heard the man," Gabriel said at last, returning his attention to the whipped cream. "Kendra, can you prepare a tea tray for his guest?"

The submissive little cook looked up with wide, startled eyes, like she was on the verge of tears. She hurried into the kitchen's huge walk-in pantry, presumably in search of teabags.

She'd been terrified of Rafe since the day she started, more than three years earlier. He admittedly hadn't done much to ease that fear, liking the way she hunched in on herself whenever he entered the kitchen, trying to appear as small as possible. It always sent a thrill through him—made him feel like a predator spotting his next prey.

Now it just made him feel like an asshole. Though, for the life of him, he couldn't figure out why. It's not like he'd ever been mean to the girl. Best he could remember, he'd never even been mildly rude. What the hell did he have to feel bad about? He found himself wishing for the two cooks on Gabriel's evening staff, Sienna and Eric. They were a much hardier lot.

Holding in an annoyed growl, he waited as patiently as he could while Luca and Kendra prepared everything for him. The bulk of the tray was taken up by a vintage porcelain teapot with matching cup and saucer, plus sugar cubes, tongs, and a tiny silver spoon. There was also a small wooden box Kendra assured him contained twenty different flavors of tea, her trembling voice barely even a whisper.

Spread around the four corners were three cups of fancy iced tea lattes; the bright green one was apparently called a matcha latte, but the rest went in one ear and out the other. And then, of course, his own coffee, tucked into the fourth corner.

"Wow," he said, staring down at the tea smorgasbord. "This is amazing, Kendra. Thank you."

Once again, all eyes in the kitchen were glued to his face. Jesus, maybe he had been an asshole, whether he meant to be or not.

"Y-you're welcome, Sir," she whispered, scurrying back to her station.

Making a mental note to say thank you more often, Rafe stalked out of the room, barely sparing a glance at the two still enjoying their breakfast in the dining room. He knew from the start his week with Nell would force him out of his comfort zone. But it was already so much more than he imagined, and they were only on day three.

The weirdest part was, he wasn't even sure how he felt about it. At least part of him *liked* the way she made him feel off balance. Like maybe it had been a long time coming.

Rafe got most of the way down the back hallway before he heard it —the sound of someone's rapid, desperate gasps for air.

"*Fuck.*"

He ran the rest of the way to the parlor, various teas sloshing over the sides of the cups, mixing with his near-black coffee on the silver tray. Bursting in through the parlor doorway, he found Nell curled up into a tight ball on the floor, hyperventilating.

"Hey," he said, dropping the tray on an end table and hurrying to her side. "It's all right. I'm h—"

A bloodcurdling scream cut off his words. He'd tried to pull her hands away from her face, and she wrenched away from him as though his touch burned her skin.

Panic swelling in his own chest, he knelt down on the rug beside her, getting as close as he could without touching her. If she went into attack mode and succeeded in breaking his nose this time, so fucking be it. She had to know she wasn't alone.

"I'm here," he said, doing his best to project a sense of calm and peace with his voice. "I'm not going anywhere."

Footsteps pounded down the hall, and he looked up as Mason skidded to a stop in the doorway. But he waved the other man away. Nell didn't need help from a total stranger right now. She needed *him*.

"Whatever happened, I'll help you through it," he whispered as Mason backed away, his eyes sharp with interest. "You don't have to do this alone anymore. I'll make sure you don't ever have to do this alone again—not if I can help it."

He kept up a steady stream of soothing words, not even sure she could hear him, but at a complete loss for what else to do. At last, after what felt like a literal eternity, she stopped hyperventilating, though her wracking sobs continued for another couple of minutes.

When all was quiet and still, Rafe tentatively placed a hand on her shoulder. This time, she leaned into his touch, and that was all the permission he needed. Gathering her up into his arms, he held her tight against his chest, burying a hand in her hair. She folded into his warmth like a cat curling up in a sunbeam.

"What happened, kitten?"

It was several long seconds before she whispered back, "I got an email from Holly."

Oh, fuck. If Holly rejected her, and his plan made everything worse, he'd never forgive himself. Trying to keep the guilt out of his voice, he asked, "What did she say?"

She nuzzled her face against his chest with a little sniff. "I haven't opened it yet. I only saw the preview, but it doesn't . . ." She took a moment to compose herself before finishing. "It doesn't look good."

Rafe squinted toward the laptop screen, but the tiny words were nothing more than a blur from so far away. "You'll never know for sure unless you actually read it," he told her, using the same calming voice from before. "How can I help?"

"Read it to me?" Her voice was so fragile and small, like a child's. It killed him that his actions, his plan, brought her to this state.

"Of course." He didn't want to jostle her by moving closer to the laptop, and he'd never be able to hold it and scroll with her in his lap. So instead, he grabbed hold of the intricately carved wood along the base of the sofa, dragging the whole thing toward them.

He had a feeling three of the partners—Jonathan, Aiden, and Leo—would kill him if they ever found out about his rough handling of their precious antique. Especially Aiden. The dude had a serious hard-on for old, fancy woodwork.

Then again, considering there wasn't a Dom in the place who hadn't fucked a naked woman on that sofa, they could get the fuck over it.

"Okay," he said, finding the email from Holly Campbell and clicking on it. "No matter what happens, try to remember the end goal. Whole new beautiful you."

"Right. Caterpillars go through all sorts of messy shit before they get to be butterflies." She tried for, and failed to achieve, a front of bravado. "Let's get this over with."

Heart pounding with a nervousness he wasn't remotely used to feeling, he began to read out loud.

Noelle,

You've got to be fucking kidding me. Nine years, ten months, and three days. That's how long it's been since we last talked. That's how long I've been waiting, checking this stupid email address every single day, on the off chance you ever reached out. That's how long I've felt like half of me was missing. How long I've had to wonder if you were even alive.

You're telling me it's been more than a year since you left that asshole? I could've talked to you last October? I could've been with you, helping you, rebuilding your life with you? And you made me wait a whole extra year because you thought I was mad at you?

OF COURSE I FUCKING WANT TO SEE YOU. Oh my fucking God, I can't believe I even had to type that. You're one of the smartest people I've ever known, but you've never had a lick of common sense. I guess some things never change :P

Send me your phone number as soon as you can. I have to hear your voice. I have to know it's really you. That you're really okay.

We have so much time to make up for. And goddamnit, we're going to make up for every single second we missed. That's a fucking promise.

With all my love (seriously, I'll always love you, you dumb bitch),

Holly

P.S. You're an aunt now. I'll tell you all about Justin and his daddy when we talk.

P.P.S. I fucking love you.

He read straight through the letter without pause, not wanting to keep her in even a moment of suspense. But he'd felt her slowly uncurl the more he read. As soon as the last word passed through his lips, he looked down at the woman in his lap.

Tears streamed down Nell's cheeks again, but this time, she had the most radiant smile he'd ever seen in his life. The pure joy on her face made his chest swell up so much, it was actually painful. He felt like the fucking Grinch, his heart growing three sizes all at once.

It wasn't necessarily a bad feeling. But it was sure as hell an odd one.

For one thing, he found himself understanding Aiden like never before. No wonder he liked to help damaged, lost little subs find their way. Nothing Rafe had done up to this point in his life felt as good as this moment, right here.

But that begged one very obvious question—what in the fuck was he going to do next?

CHAPTER 9
Nell

Nell fiddled with the hem of her dress as she stared at Rafe's phone, her eyes glazed over. Which meant she nearly jumped out of her skin when it finally rang in her hand.

Heart pounding against her ribs, she stared down at the little screen. "It says 'unknown number.' Do you think that's her, or spam?"

Rafe, who had moved to the sofa and planted her on his lap half an hour ago, squeezed her thigh. "Only one way to find out."

Her finger hovered over the green button, but she couldn't make herself actually press down. Fucking hell, she couldn't even breathe. What if it was Holly, and she never called again? It wasn't like Nell could call her back without the number. *Press the fucking button!*

Coming to her rescue, Rafe gently pushed her thumb down, sliding it across the screen to answer the call. He hit the speakerphone button a moment later. But he wouldn't speak for her. He told her that as soon as he gave her his phone.

If only he would. Nell's voice was stuck somewhere in her throat, and she wasn't sure it would ever break loose.

After several terrifying seconds, a strong, confident voice blared from the phone's speakers. "Hello? Noelle?" Three more beats of silence, in which Nell started to accept she'd likely be mute for the rest of her life. "If this is someone playing a trick on me, I hope you know you're going to burn in the deepest ring of hell for all eternity. And if this is Micah O'Neill, I swear to God and fucking Jesus that I will castrate you before the day I die, and you will be fully conscious and aware while I do it. You can fucking count on it."

A laugh bubbled up out of Nell as tears burned in her eyes. Fucking hell, Holly hadn't changed one tiny bit, and it was the most wonderful goddamn thing in the world. She could even feel Rafe shaking with silent laughter behind her.

"Holy shit, Noelle!" The relief in Holly's voice tore through her, lodging itself in the deepest chambers of her heart. Christ, she'd never be able to forgive herself for what she put everyone through. "Is it really you? Please say it's really you, cause I can't take much more of this."

"It's really me."

Nell could barely even hear her own voice, but it was enough. Holly promptly burst into very loud and very Holly-ish tears. Her older sister had never done anything halfway.

"Please tell me this is real." It was hard to make out her words through all the gasping and crying and hiccupping. "Tell me he's not standing behind you making you do this."

By this point, Nell was practically sobbing too, and it took her several seconds to compose herself enough to answer. Taking the phone off speaker, she moved it up to her ear. "I really did leave him. I promise. I haven't seen or spoken to him in over a year, like I said." It was technically true. She read his email, but she hadn't responded.

"Thank fucking God." Holly's voice grew more distant as she spoke, and then came the muffled sound of a nose blowing. When next she spoke, her voice came through loud and clear. "Okay, I need to know everything. Where are you? What have you been doing for the last year? When can I see you? Are you coming home?"

Head spinning from the rapid-fire questions, Nell took a deep breath and answered as best she could. "I've been living in Tampa since I left. I got a job bartending at a club. I have a nice apartment, and I've been slowly putting my life back together." She paused, not sure how to answer any of the rest. "I—I don't know about coming home. That depends."

"On?"

Swallowing down the fear rising up in her throat, she whispered, "On whether anyone other than you ever wants to see me again."

Holly made a sound so sad, so pitying, it made Nell want to cry again. "Oh, honey. *Everyone* will want to see you."

"Even Mom and Dad?" They hadn't wanted to see her ever since they found out about the nature of her relationship with Micah. Neither even bothered to attend the intervention, though Holly begged them to come.

It was several telling seconds before her sister finally answered. "I'll convince them. Give me a little time."

Since Nell wasn't exactly chomping at the bit to face her parents anytime soon, that was an easy thing to give. Nothing in the world filled her with more shame than knowing what she put them through. Knowing that *they knew* she willingly handed over all her personal power to a monster, becoming his slave of her own free will. No matter what Holly said, she didn't think they'd ever truly understand.

"I just saw Cady and Ben a couple weeks ago, though. I know for a fucking fact they want to see you."

Nell's mouth dropped open. "Wait, you did? Why?"

"Cady moved back to the Seattle area after grad school, and Ben came back after he and his wife had their second kid a few years ago. They wanted to be closer to his parents. We try to get together once a month. It helps. Almost like our own little support group."

Feeling like she'd been hit upside the head with a two by four, Nell took a moment to process that. Ben was married? He was a *father*? All at once, the postscript from Holly's email struck her anew, and she blurted out, "Shit, you're married now, too. And a mom! I want to know everything."

Nell spent the next hour listening to Holly tell her everything she missed in the last near-decade. Joy and sorrow flooded through her in equal measure, to know the people she loved were living such beautiful, happy lives—and to know she missed every single bit of it. If Rafe hadn't been a solid, constant presence through the whole thing, his arms wrapped tight around her middle, she wouldn't have made it through all the revelations without breaking down.

It had always been a given that Nell and Holly would be the maids of honor in each other's weddings. But Nell not only missed her sister's big day—she'd never even met the groom. It was somehow worse to know she'd been an aunt for three and a half years without meeting her nephew once.

Ben married a doctor he met in med school, and they now had three (fucking *three*) kids. Cady got married only months ago, to an English Lit professor at UDub—a British woman named Cynthia who had, it seemed, quite literally swept her off her feet.

She hadn't been there for her friends. Not for any of it.

As for their parents, Holly hesitated to say anything until Nell pressed the issue. Reluctantly, she admitted, "Mom took down all the pictures of you in the house. They freak out whenever anyone mentions you, so we all stopped trying a long time ago. Just to keep the peace."

"They wish I didn't exist." It hurt less than she expected to say it. Probably because it wasn't remotely surprising.

"Yeah, well, I'm changing that." Only Holly could make such an impossible claim with so much confidence. "I'll get started right away. Pete and I can have them over for dinner as soon as they're free."

Nell arched her brows. "You think Pete'll actually be on my side?" She'd heard plenty about Holly's husband in the last hour. The guy sounded like the perfect partner for her sister—laid-back enough to put up with her exuberance and crazy schemes, but strong enough not to be bulldozed.

Holly never said a thing to indicate how he felt about his MIA sister-in-law, though.

Scoffing, Holly said, "Of course he's on your side, Noelle. He gave me the biggest fucking hug when I showed him your email this morning. He knows how important you are to me."

For what felt like the thousandth time that morning, Nell was crying. "I actually go by Nell now. If that's okay."

"Of course it's okay. You can go by whatever the fuck you want." After a pause, Holly added, "Though I hope it's not because that piece of shit told you to."

"The opposite, actually. Whenever someone said Noelle in their Dom voice, it made me think of him. Mistress Freya, my new boss, helped me come up with a nickname I loved so I stopped having so many panic attacks."

Another long pause, and Nell held her breath. Moment of truth.

Holly's voice was carefully neutral when she said, "So you're still doing the BDSM stuff." It wasn't a question.

At least she didn't sound angry. Matching her sister's bland tone, Nell said, "The club I work at in Tampa is called Valhalla. It's a BDSM club."

She braced for anger, yelling, accusations. So it came as one hell of a shock when, instead, her sister stayed completely and utterly calm, like the surface of a pond on a windless day. "Tell me more."

It had been a hell of a lot easier to listen to Holly talk than to do it herself. But she knew her sister deserved to know all about her current situation. Rebuilding the trust she broke started and ended with the truth.

Holly stayed silent as Nell filled her in, beginning with the day she left Micah. The way a pawn shop owner cut the thin gold collar off her neck since only Micah had a key. Using the money to buy a bus ticket to Florida. Her bug-infested, pay-by-the-week motel room—the only thing she could afford with the meager tips from her waitressing job. The way Mistress Freya came into the all-night diner with several of her staff at three AM one Saturday, and by the end of the night decided to take Nell under her wing. How much she loved her boss, her job, her new apartment.

Then, with a deep breath to settle her nerves, she finished with, "Mistress Freya is helping me get back into the lifestyle. She knows it's what I need, but also knows how fucked up I am after everything that happened. How scared I've been of the whole thing happening all over again." Warning bells went off in her head, telling her to stop talking, but Holly deserved the *whole* truth. "She found me someone who she trusts. Someone I can trust."

Holly's disappointed sigh just about broke her fucking heart. *Please, please, please.* She repeated the word over and over in her head as she waited, desperate for her sister not to reject her so soon after getting her back.

"You're not doing that whole slave thing again, are you?" Holly asked at last.

"No!" She hadn't meant to shout the word, but it came flying out of her. "Holly, I give you my fucking word, I'm *never* doing full-time power exchange again. Never, ever, *ever*. I'm only staying here for a week, and it's nothing like that."

Rafe tightened his arms around her, planting a soft kiss in her hair, and the gesture calmed the thoughts racing through her mind.

Nell couldn't imagine the strength of will it took her sister to sound supportive when she said, "Tell me about him."

"Well, his name's Rafe—"

"Rafe? Like Ralph Fiennes?"

"Yeah, but actually spelled like it sounds. And he's *way* better looking than Voldemort."

Holly and Rafe both laughed at that, though Holly's cut off abruptly. "Oh my God, is he there with you?"

"You're not on speaker," Nell rushed to assure her. "He's just here for moral support, I swear. He's the one I told you about in my email—the person who's helping me reach out to the people I love and get my shit together. He's even got me doing career research."

No one could ever think he was like Micah after hearing that. And yet, the seconds ticked by as Nell waited for a response. Fuck, should she have told Holly from the start that Rafe was with her? Was this yet another betrayal of her trust?

At last, Holly admitted, "I guess I can't be mad. If Pete wasn't on Justin duty right now, he'd be here with me, too. But it's hard to have a conversation longer than ten seconds with a toddler around."

Nell breathed a relieved sigh. "I promise you haven't been on speaker. Not except for the first thirty seconds or so."

"The first thirty seconds, you say?" There was a new note of mischief in her voice. "Put me back on speaker."

One corner of Nell's lips twitched. She had no idea what her sister was up to, but she had a feeling it would be entertaining as hell. Pulling the phone away from her ear, she tapped the speaker button again.

"Rafe?" Holly said, imperious as a queen.

"I'm pleased to meet you, Holly," he said in that gruff, sexy voice of his.

"Mmm." She didn't bother to hide her skepticism. "My sister tells me you heard the first thirty seconds of our call."

Rafe didn't seem at all phased by her tone. "Nell needed a little help getting started, that's all."

"Well, if you heard what I said, then you know what I'm willing to do to men who hurt my sister." After a dramatic pause, she finished with, "I highly suggest you don't if you want your balls to remain attached to your body."

Wincing, Nell twisted around in his lap so she could look up at him, worried the threat would make him mad. It certainly would've sent Brian or Micah flying off the handle. But the only word she could think of to describe his smile was *feral*.

"I'm going to hold you to that, Holly Campbell. Whether it's me or any other man. Though from what I can tell, Nell's perfectly capable of cutting off my balls herself."

Her sister's surprised laughter made all the tension melt out of Nell's shoulders, and she leaned her head back against Rafe's chest. For the first time in so many years, she finally felt like everything might truly turn out okay. So long as she kept trying.

CHAPTER 10

Rafe

I t was easy to see why Nell worshipped her sister so much. The woman was a force to be reckoned with, and Rafe believed she was at least half serious about the whole castration thing. God help Micah O'Neill if the man ever saw Holly again. Not that the asshole deserved protection, celestial or otherwise.

Nell asked to stay in his lap after ending her phone call with her sister. Given how incredibly fucking brave she'd been, it seemed only right to grant the simple request. Holly straight-up ordered Nell to email her high school best friends, passing on their up-to-date contact info along with her own, but he'd been watching her struggle to compose emails to Cady and Ben for the last forty minutes.

"I think those are perfect," he said, after watching her change a word for the fourth time. In fact, he was almost sure she put it back to what it was originally. "You have a beautiful way with words."

The loveliest blush colored her cheeks. "You don't think it's too beautiful, do you? My agent used to send me scripts for the shittiest TV show pilots. Stuff with dialogue so unnatural I knew the show would never get greenlit. This has to sound *real*. I want Ben and Cady to think this legit came from the heart, not that I'm trying to—"

"Nell."

Her babble ended at the merest hint of his Dom voice. "Yes, Sir?"

"Hit send."

She relaxed against him, her head resting on his shoulder, and did as she was told. "Thank you."

"My pleasure. Are you done with your tasks for today?"

"There's one more thing I want to do," she answered, surprising him. Sending those emails put her up to three points, and he expected her to be talking about her next fantasy by now.

But that surprise was nothing compared to what hit him when she typed *How to become a therapist* into the search bar. He watched with brows arched as high as they would go while she navigated through the results, adding info to her New Dream Job document now and again. This was a much deeper dive into a specific career path than she did yesterday, and therapist hadn't even been on her list.

When at last she saved and closed the document, Nell twisted around in his lap to look up at him. "I'm finished, Sir."

He knew he shouldn't pry. Her task was to do the research and figure out a new path for her life, not explain herself to him. But he couldn't stop himself from saying, "A therapist, huh?"

She blushed again, but excitement sparked in her eyes. "Something Holly said made me think of it." She spoke a little faster than normal, with a passion he found hypnotizing. "About how she and Ben both spent a long time in therapy after the intervention, working through their anger and grief and fear and all that. And it got me thinking about how much I could've used a therapist this last year. How maybe the Mistress might not have needed to rope you into doing her such a huge favor—"

"I hope you don't think that's why I'm doing this," he interrupted. It may have been the only reason he agreed to take her as a guest, but it sure as fuck wasn't the reason for anything that happened since. "I'm doing this for *you*, not Freya."

Her small smile told him she thought that very thing and was beyond pleased to hear otherwise. "Anyway," she said, her voice a little softer but her excitement in no way diminished. "If I'd found a therapist who really understood the way my brain works, what my body needs, how I feel about everything—someone who won't judge me because they seriously get me . . . maybe I could've started healing a long time ago. Hell, if I went to one sooner, maybe I never would've gotten myself into the situation with Micah in the first place."

"And you want to be that person for other people?" He didn't bother keeping the pride and admiration out of his voice. She deserved to know she earned it.

"Without Mistress Freya, without you? I'd be a fucking mess. But what if the Mistress hadn't come into the diner that night? What if I never met either of you? God only knows what kind of state I'd be in right now." Squaring her shoulders, she finished with, "No one should have to go through what I did alone."

Grabbing hold of her face, Rafe slammed his mouth down over hers. Her lips parted without a fight, giving his tongue access to explore, to taste, to control.

And he fucking *devoured* her. Like his executioner was pounding on the door, and she was his last meal.

Rafe tossed the laptop onto the sofa, gripping her hips and twisting her around so her legs straddled his. When she lifted her arms toward the ceiling, he wasn't about to pass up the invitation. He broke the kiss only long enough to yank her dress up over her head, then went right back to claiming her mouth as he tossed the garment aside.

Christ, she felt so fucking good in his hands. Her long, lean torso, the flare of her hips, that delectable, oh-so-spankable ass. He raked his fingernails across the lace of her panties. How fucking dare something keep him from touching her skin. Growling into her mouth, he ripped them clean off her body, her yelp making his cock jerk.

"Please," she begged, her lips brushing against his, her breath hot against his face.

He buried his hands in her hair and rasped out, "Please what?"

"Please may I touch you, Sir?"

Her answer surprised him so much, he jerked her back by her hair, needing to look into her eyes. He'd expected her to say *touch me* or *fuck me*, or something else along those lines. Something purely sexual, and not quite so . . . *intimate*.

Nell watched him with such raw need written all over her face, it took his breath away. Because it wasn't simply lust he saw lurking in the depths of her eyes, though there was plenty of that. He saw a desperation to please him, to connect with him on as deep a level as possible—to become his in a way no woman had for years.

And it scared the ever-loving shit out of him.

"Lace your hands on the back of your head." His tone left no room for argument. As she complied, he undid his belt and pants with rapid jerks of his fingers. Lifting his hips with her still on top of them put enough pressure on the back of the sofa to make the antique creak ominously. Not wanting Aiden to murder him, he dropped back onto the blue velvet as soon as he pushed his jeans and boxers down enough for his cock to spring free.

Shifting her hips forward, Nell raised herself up on her knees, dragging her smooth pussy up the length of his cock. He took hold of her as he moaned, his large hands digging into her hips and ass, holding her in place.

"Who's in control here?" he demanded.

"You are, Sir." Though she didn't sound remotely apologetic for her actions.

"Then fucking act like it," he ground out, lifting her up, positioning her pussy directly over his cock. She was so fucking wet that he entered her in one thrust, without the slightest resistance.

Nell threw back her head and moaned, her arms shaking with the strain of holding them up for so long. Loving the way she suffered for him, he said, "Keep those elbows back," as he lifted her, slamming her down onto him again.

Her arms shot back, forcing her chest out, practically presenting her breasts for his inspection. Christ, that red bustier was sexy. But he didn't want satin and lace between them, blocking him, hiding her from his gaze. Undoing the hooks up the back with swift precision, he tossed the garment aside.

With another growl, he captured one hardened nipple in his mouth, relishing the way it stretched and pulled as he continued to fuck her. He had to catch the stiff bud in his teeth to keep it from popping out of his mouth entirely, and she cried out at the sharp pain.

Releasing her nipple at last, he ordered, "Ride me, kitten. Use your legs." He kept one hand on her hip, helping her balance as her thighs and ass worked, pumping her up and down on his cock.

For several long seconds, the flex and shift of her muscles mesmerized him. Jesus fucking Christ, she was strong. He was an avid gym rat, and knew how much work she must've put in. It made his cock hard as fucking stone.

Once she developed her own steady rhythm, he lifted his second hand to her mouth, pushing two fingers between her lips. "Suck."

She clamped her lips around the digits before he even spoke, laving them with her tongue. It made a wet popping noise when he yanked his hand away, lowering his fingers to her clit. Her whole body shuddered at the first slippery contact.

With a grin he knew was downright evil, he said, "Don't just ride my cock, you little slut. Ride my fingers. Make yourself come." He kept his hand perfectly still, forcing her to do all the work.

Whimpering, she did as she was told, moving herself up and down on his cock, rolling her hips forward on each descent. There was a look of intense concentration on her face, her eyes screwed shut so tight she'd probably have a fucking headache by the time they were done.

One particularly slow and enthusiastic roll of her hips had his eyes rolling back in his head. "*Sweet fuck.*"

She buried her face in his neck as she came, screaming as her pussy clenched around him, forcing him over the edge whether he wanted it or not.

When Nell finally stopped panting for breath, she pulled away with a dreamy smile. "I didn't even tell you my fantasy yet, and you already made me see stars."

"That one was for free. We've still got four more to go." He planted a kiss on the tip of her nose. "And speaking of, why don't you tell me what you want today."

A speculative look stole into her eyes, and she nibbled on her lower lip as she considered. It made him want to catch that lip between his own teeth, to suck and bite until she begged for mercy, but he restrained himself.

When at last she answered him, she sounded on edge—even a little afraid. "I don't know how to ask for what I want."

Frowning down at her, he said, "You have to know by now I won't judge you."

Her gaze skittered away. "You might judge me for this," she muttered under her breath.

Taking firm hold of her chin, he held her in place until she looked at him again. "I read your application. I've seen your limit list. Nothing you say will surprise me." When she still didn't answer, he used the cold, commanding voice that always had such an immediate effect. "Now, Nell. Don't keep me waiting any longer."

"Butterfly." It came out as a terrified whisper.

Rafe let go of her chin as if it had burned him. Christ, she was still on top of him, his cock buried deep inside her. He had no fucking clue what he should to do. Lift her off him? Sit back and stay still until she disengaged and moved away?

"I'm sorry," she said, scurrying away, his softening cock slipping out of her as she went. She curled up into a ball in one of the armchairs, her knees tucked up under her chin. "I shouldn't have said it. It's just a question. Fuck, fuck, *fuck*, I'm so fucking stupid. It's not like you're hurting me. I can't believe I'm so—"

"Nell, what did I say about apologizing?" Rafe interrupted, wanting to stop her before she worked herself up even more. While he waited for an answer, he sat up and got his jeans back in order.

She took half a dozen long, slow breaths before finally meeting his eyes again. "Not to apologize unless you told me to."

"Good girl," he said, leaning forward, his forearms resting on his thighs. "Did I ask you to apologize for using your safeword?"

She shook her head. "No, Sir."

"That's because you're allowed to use it for whatever reason you want." He did his best to sound patient and understanding, when in reality, he was burning to know what fantasy upset her so much. "There's only one rule when it comes to safewords. If you want what we're doing to stop, say it. I'm never going to get mad, no matter what we're doing."

She watched him for several long seconds, as if she expected him to change his mind. When all he did was look back at her with a mild expression, she whispered, "Do you promise?"

The fear and uncertainty in her voice made his chest ache. "I promise."

After another few beats, she unfurled her arms and legs, sitting up straight. "So I don't have to tell you that fantasy? I can tell you a different one?"

"You can tell me whatever fantasy you want."

She considered that for several seconds, the ideas flashing bright in her eyes. When she spoke, she still sounded uncertain. "Would you sell me into sexual slavery?"

It took every bit of self-control he possessed to keep the shock off his face. Doing all he could to keep the surprise from altering his voice, as well, he said, "Give me more info."

He must've done a piss-poor job, because she winced. "See? I knew you'd judge me. And that's not even the bad one."

Rafe had no clue what to do with that statement. "I'm not judging," he assured her. "I'm just a little . . . surprised. After everything you've been through—"

"I don't want anything like what I had with Micah." There was so much fire in her voice, he couldn't bring himself to scold her for interrupting. "This is just a fantasy. A scene. I've read so many books and stories about girls being auctioned off. In contemporary books, like at high-end sex clubs or secret sex societies. Or in historical romance, like a slave market in Ancient Greece or whatever. Hell, it's even in alien smut. And I know it's fucked up, but even after Micah, I still think about it when I make myself come. If that makes me stupid, so be it." She glared at him by the time she finished.

Rafe's expression softened all on its own. "It's not fucked up, Nell. And you're not stupid. Not even a little bit."

Tears leaked out of the corners of her eyes, and he hated himself for making her feel like this.

"Listen to me." Moving to stand in front of her, he wiped the tears away with his thumbs. "You're not even close to the first sub within these walls to have that fantasy, and I assure you that you won't be the last. You have nothing to be ashamed of." A lightbulb went off over his head then, and he asked, "When did you start having this fantasy?"

"I don't know," she said with a forlorn, one-shouldered shrug.

"When I was nineteen or twenty, maybe? I was definitely dating Brian at the time."

"Then that makes all the sense in the world. You had a fantasy you tried to make into reality with Micah. But he twisted it all out of shape until it was nothing like what you dreamed of." He ran his fingers through her hair, and she closed her eyes with a soft sigh. "Of course you still have the fantasy. It's never been fulfilled."

Her hands fluttered like she wanted to reach up and touch him, but fell back to her sides. "Do you really mean that?" she whispered.

"I do. I swear on my honor, as a card-carrying member of the Dominance, Intercourse, Control, and Kink Society, everything I just said is true."

She reared back, mirth dancing in her eyes. "The Dominance, Intercourse, Control, and Kink Society?" Laughing, she added, "The D.I.C.K.S.? Seriously?"

"I must admit, I made that up." Jesus, he was smiling again. He was going to get a lot more fucking wrinkles at this rate. "But it should exist, don't you think? And then you can join the American Society of Submissives, or A.S.S. for short."

"Dicks and ass," she said, wiggling her eyebrows. "One of my favorite combinations."

Eh, fuck it. He'd be forty in less than a year. He was supposed to have wrinkles. Grinning like an absolute fool, he said, "Now tell me more about this slave auction of yours."

CHAPTER 11
Nell

Had those eye hooks on the ceiling always been there? Nell found herself staring at them as Rafe led her into the dining room. The table was gone, and all the chairs faced a small, raised platform in front of the windows. The stainless-steel plates of the eye hooks were screwed into the ceiling on either side of the platform, a heavy silver chain dangling from each one.

Nell tripped over the edge of the Persian rug, pitching forward toward the back row of chairs. She instinctively tried to throw her hands out to her sides for balance, but Rafe bound her hands in front of her before they left the suite, using thick leather cuffs hooked to a metal ring.

It was a good thing Rafe caught her. Bashing her head open on a straight back wooden chair would certainly put a damper on things.

"Careful, girl," Rafe grunted, punctuating the words with a single stroke from his rattan cane. He used enough force to get her attention, but not to make her cry out.

A delicious shiver ran through her body, making her pussy ache with need. "I'm sorry, Master."

Letting the cane's wrapped grip fall from his hand, the long rod dangled from the nylon cord around his wrist. He took her upper arm in an iron grip. "If you do something to damage yourself and lower your value, I swear you won't see tomorrow." He gave her a long leer up and down the length of her body. With a sound of disgust, he dragged her the rest of the way across the room. "Up, you little slut."

She stumbled again as she climbed onto the platform, Rafe's fist in her hair the only thing keeping her from toppling off the far side.

"Clumsy little bitch," he spat, spinning her around to face the chairs. "I'll be relieved to see the last of you."

Rafe unhooked the leather cuffs, pocketing the ring he'd used to connect them, and stretched her right arm toward the first chain. While he busied himself with attaching the cuff to one of the thick links, she took a look around the room.

More people arrived in the last couple of minutes, filling all the seats. She recognized Camden from the scene yesterday, in the back row. She'd seen a couple of the others around the Manor, but had no idea who they were.

There were even two submissives in attendance, one with disheveled black hair perched on the lap of a Dom with just the right amount of sexy stubble, her legs splayed to either side of his while he toyed with her pussy. She had what looked like some kind of monochrome flower tattooed on her arm.

The other was a stunning woman with white-blond hair in an elaborate up-do, kneeling at the feet of a tall, lean Dom in a perfectly tailored gray suit. A leather collar was buckled around her neck, matching the leash attached to a thick silver ring. The Dom ran the other end of the leash absentmindedly through his hands as he studied Nell.

Squeezing her thighs together, she tried to relieve some of the ache in her pussy, to no avail. Rafe had offered to introduce her to the other Manor Doms before the auction, but she'd turned him down without hesitation. She didn't want to know a thing about the man who bought her when it happened. That was one of the most important parts of the fantasy.

All she needed to know was that she'd be safe the entire time—and that she'd be back with Rafe once the scene ended.

Soon, both arms were stretched wide, her shoulders strained, her feet not quite able to rest flat on the platform. For a few, magical seconds, she closed her eyes, imagining herself on the stage in the Domino Club—a secret society featured in several of her favorite books.

They auctioned off a different woman at the beginning of each novel, always bought by a stunningly sexy Dom who had no problem disciplining her whenever she misbehaved. Nell first devoured the series in college, and it had been at the foundation of this fantasy ever since.

"Gentlemen, welcome," Rafe said, drawing her back to the present. She opened her eyes to find everyone in the room staring raptly at the stage. "The auction will start in only a few minutes. But before we begin, I'd like to open the floor to any questions."

"How old is the slave?" asked the man with the woman on his lap.

With a polite nod, Rafe said, "Thirty-six. I've tested her out myself, and she still has plenty of wear left in her. I give you my word."

Camden leaned back in his chair and asked, "How long has she been in your possession?"

"Only three days."

Eyebrows shot up all over the room. It was the Dom with the leash who asked what everyone was thinking: "And you're already selling? What's wrong with her?"

"Gentlemen." Rafe smiled, spreading his hands wide. "Do you not remember what it said in the invite? I'm selling a slave with a strong will who needs a heavy hand. I lack the time or patience to train her myself right now, but I know she'll be a perfect project for one of you. She just needs to be broken."

It was a good thing Rafe dressed her up in black lace panties and a matching corset, or there would surely be an embarrassingly large puddle on the floor beneath her.

"Does she take punishment well?" That came from the fifth and final Dom in the room—one she'd never seen before today.

"How about a short demonstration, and you can decide for yourself?" Rafe suggested. At the murmurs of assent around the room, he dragged her panties down to her upper thighs, then once again took up his rattan cane.

The first line of fire landed across the center of her ass. *Fuuuuuuuck.* How she managed to say it in her head and not out loud was a mystery for the ages. This stroke was a whole shit ton harder than the warning shot he gave her a few minutes earlier, and without even the skimpy panties to protect her.

Rafe's second stroke fell parallel to the first, and her vision blurred with unshed tears. Wielded with enough force, a cane could tear through the skin, slicing its target to ribbons. She knew he was far too controlled to let that happen, but god-fucking-damnit, it fucking *hurt*.

"I'll let them see you take one more," Rafe said, using the cane to mark out a spot directly below the second stripe. When the cane fell, his aim was perfect, and a third line of fire burned across her skin.

Tears poured from her eyes, but she never made a sound.

The Dom holding the black-haired woman in his lap let out a long, jagged breath. "Beautiful."

Rafe's smile could only be described as victorious. "If there are no more questions?" When no one said a word, he slid her panties back up into place, making her hiss as rough lace settled on her punished bottom. "Very well, then. Who would like to start the bidding?"

"Five hundred," Camden bellowed, and when their gazes met, he winked at her.

Nell glanced down at the rug in front of her, trying her damndest not to laugh. She'd have to avoid looking at him for the rest of the scene, or he could derail the whole thing.

"A thousand," the one with the black-haired girl in his lap countered.

The Dom with the leash lazily raised one hand. "Fifteen hundred."

"Two thousand." That was the Dom who got her caned.

Deep, commanding voices continued to call out, increasingly absurd numbers ringing in the otherwise silent room. Nell's head swung from side to side as she tried to keep track, her heart skipping a beat at each new bid.

"Sold to Mason St. John, for fifteen thousand dollars." There was a tremendous amount of smugness in Rafe's voice, as if he just pulled off the deal of the century. It made her long to go to him, to beg him to buy her back—to earn his regard in whatever way he required, no matter how painful or humiliating.

But it was too late for that. Mason stood from his spot near the kitchen door, laying his sub's leash on the floor in front of her knees.

"Gemma, stay." The other sub didn't move anything but her eyes, tracking Mason as he sauntered toward the platform.

Well, Nell certainly couldn't complain about how sexy her new "Master" was. Though she admittedly had a fleeting thought he would've been better suited for her fantasy yesterday. The suit and glasses made him look more like a sexy professor than anything else.

But no, not with those cheekbones. He looked like he belonged on a runway, not in a classroom.

He made a slow circle around the platform, examining every inch of her, searching for defects in his new property. When he made it to where Rafe waited patiently, the two Doms shook hands.

"Always a pleasure doing business with you," Rafe said. "Would you like me to deliver her to your suite later? Or—"

"No, I'd prefer to take possession now." Pulling a checkbook and fountain pen from the inside pocket of his jacket, Mason wrote out the topmost check, signing it with a flourish. As he handed it to Rafe, she could just see the small *15,000.00* written in the little box next to the dollar sign. "Gemma, come."

The blond sub crawled across the dining room toward him, her leash trailing through the valley of her breasts and down between her legs. Nell couldn't tear her eyes away from the woman. Her garter harness matched the collar and leash, all buckles, silver rings, and black leather straps, hugging the curves of her old Hollywood hourglass shape to absolute distraction. Every inch of her was visible under her sheer black bra and panties.

But all of that was eclipsed by the almost feline way she crawled. She may well have been the sexiest woman Nell had ever seen.

When Gemma knelt up at Mason's feet, he cupped her cheek tenderly. "You'll be a good girl for me if I remove your collar, won't you?"

She leaned into his hand, her eyes fluttering closed. "Of course, Master," she whispered.

"Good girl." Unfastening Gemma's collar, Mason turned and buckled it around Nell's neck instead, tight enough to press incessantly against her throat. She swallowed, loving the short burst of pain.

As soon as Mason stepped away from the platform, Rafe got to work unhooking her cuffs from the chains. Her right shoulder screamed as she finally lowered her arm, and she rolled it a few times, trying to ease the pain.

She didn't get a chance to do the same with her other shoulder, though. The moment the cuff was free, Mason yanked on the leash, jerking her off the platform. She tumbled into him, crashing against his chest, unable to stop the, "*Shit!*" that forced its way out.

Gripping her by the shoulders, his fingertips digging painfully into her skin, Mason pushed her out to arm's length. He looped one finger through the large ring on her collar, then wrapped her hair around his other fist.

Nell cried out when he wrenched her hair, forcing her to arch her neck back as far as it could go. Her eyes widened when he leaned over her, his face as placid as ever, but his eyes filled with cold fury.

"No property of mine will speak that way," Mason said, his words like ice cutting into her skin. "The next time you do, you won't be able to sit for a week. Do I make myself clear?"

"Y-yes, Master." Jesus, this guy was intense. Wasn't Rafe supposed to be the scary one? She stumbled upon a subreddit devoted to the Manor when she researched the place, and that's what the former guests all said.

Mason's deep blue eyes bore down on her, making her want to shrink away. "Kneel."

Nell dropped to her knees without her usual grace, desperate to do whatever he said. Sitting back on her heels, she looked up at her new Master for further direction.

"Good girl. Let's go." Sparing a glance for his other sub, he said, "Gemma, come." His voice stayed low and soft, smooth as rich, melted chocolate. Nell got the distinct impression he seldom raised his voice to his subs, if ever. A man like Mason wouldn't have to.

Nell crawled after her new Master at Gemma's side, leaving the dining room and moving slowly down the long back hallway. She knew she should be concentrating on where they were going and how best to please him, but damn if she couldn't stop staring at his ass in that suit. Rafe's broader, muscled physique may have been more to her usual taste . . . didn't mean she couldn't appreciate a fine ass when she saw one.

When Mason stopped without warning, she very nearly smashed into him with her face. She would've, too, if Gemma hadn't darted a hand out, grabbing hold of her shoulder.

Luckily, he didn't notice the blunder. Only half turning, Mason unhooked the leash and gestured through an open door. "In. Both of you."

Crawling as quickly as she could into the game room, Nell yelped when the door swung closed behind her, close enough to feel the displaced air on her bare legs. She twisted around so fast she lost her balance, toppling over onto her butt.

Thank God Mason wasn't around to see *that*. He'd closed them into the room together alone.

"Is he . . ." She glanced over at Gemma, letting her confusion have free reign of her expression. "Coming back?" He'd only bought her for an hour.

Gemma's answering smile made all her worry and uncertainty melt away. "He does this. Last time, he went off somewhere to get supplies and came back in like ten minutes."

"Oh, good." She returned the other woman's smile as they stood. "I'm glad you're here so you can tell me what to expect."

With the most perfectly naughty grin Nell had ever seen, Gemma said, "Expect him to get his money's worth." She gave Nell a long, deliciously slow look down the full length of her body. "I'm so glad Master Mason bought you. He promised me someone else to play with if I was a good girl."

Mouth suddenly bone dry, Nell did her best to wet it. Her clit was quite literally pulsing. With her pale skin and white-blond hair, Gemma reminded her a little of Penny, the sub at Valhalla she had a crush on for months.

"You'd like to play with me," Gemma said, taking a few slow, prowling steps forward. "Wouldn't you?"

All Nell could manage was a needy whimper, but that seemed to be good enough for the shorter woman. Burying a hand in the hair at the nape of Nell's neck, Gemma pulled her down into a slow, achingly beautiful kiss. Where Rafe liked to claim her, practically devour her, Gemma took her time, learning the taste and shape of her mouth, swallowing each of her needy little moans.

Pulling apart only enough to speak, Gemma's lips brushed against Nell's as she whispered, "Touch me?"

She sure as fuck didn't need to be asked twice. As their lips moved back together, Nell ran her hands over Gemma's skin, exploring her incredible curves. One hand toyed with her nipple through the sheer bra, rolling and pinching as she listened to Gemma's reactions, discovering what she liked best. Still mesmerized by the garter harness, she traced a fingertip of her other hand down leather straps and around metal rings.

Nell tugged at one of the silk ribbon bows tying Gemma's panties at her hips right as the door slammed open. The two women jumped guiltily apart, the excitement in Gemma's eyes a counterpoint to the fear in Nell's. Heart in her throat, Nell faced her new Master on legs turned to lead, already knowing what she'd see.

Sure enough, Mason stood in the doorway, every muscle in his body rigid, that cold fury back in his eyes.

Fuck.

It took a few seconds for Nell to realize Gemma had knelt beside her. Dropping to her own knees, Nell stared at his chest, mind racing as she tried to figure out how much trouble she was in.

"I was gone for"—he dropped everything he carried onto the pool table and checked his ridiculously expensive looking gold watch—"six total minutes. You two couldn't keep your hands off each other for six fucking minutes?"

Blood rushed to Nell's cheeks. "I'm sorry, Master." Gemma mumbled the same beside her.

"Not as sorry as you're both about to be." Grabbing a jumble of long, thin leather straps connected by silver rings from the table, he pointed at Nell with his free hand. "You. Stand."

She did as she was told, eyeing the leather and metal contraption with trepidation. Was he going to whip her with that? She'd never seen anything like it.

It wasn't until he was buckling two straps together around the smallest part of her waist that she realized it was a garter harness, almost identical to Gemma's.

Mason's fingers were steady and sure as he fastened the buckle right above her belly button. As he worked, she reached around, finding a metal ring in the small of her back, joining the waist straps. Two additional, much shorter straps hung down the outsides of her hips, ending in more metal rings.

"Haven't you learned to keep your hands to yourself?" Mason said in a long-suffering voice, smacking her hands away.

The metal rings on her hips supported the final straps—the ones meant to go around her thighs. Mason tugged her panties down her legs, kicking them aside before he looped the remaining straps between her legs. They buckled just beneath the curve of her ass, plumping up her ass cheeks in the most fabulous way.

God, she wished she could look in a mirror. She knew she didn't have the same dramatic curves as Gemma, but if this harness made her butt look even *half* that good, she certainly wasn't opposed to the ego boost.

"Now to take care of those naughty hands," Mason said, giving her a stern look that made her insides quiver. Using the hooks on her cuffs, he attached her wrists to the harness rings on her hips, where the straps met on either side.

Unable to resist temptation, Nell tugged, finding her wrists locked in place an inch from her body. Desire raced through her, straight to her pussy and clit, and she found herself eying the riding crop Mason dropped onto the pool table. She couldn't wait to feel it biting into her tender skin.

Moving in front of Gemma, Mason took firm hold of the blonde's chin, forcing her to look up at him at what looked like a painful angle. "I expect no better of an untrained slave like Nell. But you?" His pause gave new meaning to the word *ominous*. "I'm incredibly disappointed."

"I'm so sorry, Master." Her lower lip quivered.

Leaning toward the pool table, Mason picked up the riding crop, trailing the leather slapper down the side of Gemma's face with aching slowness. Nell's pussy clenched at the sight.

"It's too late for that," Mason said, his smooth voice low and deadly.

"I planned to bring both of you so much pleasure today. But now you've forced me to punish you instead." He held her gaze for several more tense seconds, then looked down at her hands. "I don't have cuffs for you. Are you going to start being a good girl, and keep your hands to yourself from now on?"

"Yes, Master." Her voice was like liquid smoke. "Whatever you desire."

Placing the tip of the crop beneath her chin, Mason ordered, "Stand."

She rose in one perfect, fluid movement, the crop seeming to lift her from the ground. Nell found herself wondering if Gemma was a dancer, or perhaps a gymnast. She was that graceful, that beautiful.

Looking past his shoulder, Gemma locked gazes with Nell, the smoldering heat in the woman's bright green eyes almost reducing her to a puddle on the floor. Sweet fuck, she wanted both of these people. She wanted them so badly she was about to implode.

Mason made an annoyed sound deep in his throat. "I see the punishment is going to have to be severe. Let's get you both into position." Using the tip of the crop at the center of their backs, he guided first Gemma and then Nell where he wanted them, side-by-side facing one of the pool table's long edges. "Down," he ordered, pushing between Nell's shoulder blades, the edges of the stiff leather hard against her skin.

As she bent at the waist, Gemma did the same beside her. The blonde's legs were so much shorter, Nell had a feeling she was up on her toes by the time her torso touched the green wool.

"Time for these to go." Mason untied the silk ribbons at Gemma's hips, tossing aside her sheer panties.

When Mason moved up behind her, Nell felt him more than heard him. Even so, she jumped when he brushed a hand gently along the small of her back.

"These scars," he murmured, flattening his palm over the crisscrossing lines. "Did you consent to receive them?"

Her heart beat like a terrified rabbit's. Closing her eyes as tightly as she could, she forced out a strained, "No, Sir."

Mason's hand slid across her bottom, coming to rest on her right hip. "And this . . ." He traced the M, I, and partial C with a soft fingertip.

She thought back to the day Micah started to carve his name into her. He never mentioned the idea at all, so she hadn't known to fear him more than normal as he strapped her down to a table. It only became apparent how utterly fucked she was when he held a scalpel up for her to see.

She'd yelled at him. Begged him. Screamed for help she knew would never come. Needles, blades of any kind, and blood play were all at the top of her hard limits list. She kept her promise to Holly even after they stopped speaking, knowing it was a road she should never go down again. But her terror had only excited him.

If Nell hadn't left the very next morning, she had no doubt he would've finished the job. He only stopped because his cuts were so deep that she passed out from the pain. What was the fun in carving her up if she wasn't conscious to feel it?

"No, Sir." She spat out the words. "Very much *not* consensual."

"A Dominant who feels the need to brand a submissive against her will isn't any kind of Dominant at all. That motherfucker doesn't deserve anyone's submission, ever again." He made a soft humming sound as he flattened his hand over the raised letters, the warmth of his skin seeping into her. "What did you do after this happened?"

A fierce pride filled her voice when she answered, "I left. The very next day. He has no idea where I went or how to find me."

Mason moved in closer, until she could feel the bulge of his erection pressing against the crack of her ass. She hissed as the smooth fabric of his slacks brushed over the cane stripes, loving the reminder that Rafe had marked her. "There's nothing in this world more determined and powerful than a submissive. I've always thought that to be true."

Pride flashed through her like fire, heating her from the inside out. "Thank you, Master."

"You belong to me now, little Nell," he said, grinding into her, surprising a moan out of her. "But you still have your safeword as long as you're in this building. Am I correct that it's butterfly?"

"Yes, Master." God, how she wished she could push back against him. That his cock was already free of his slacks, and doing so would thrust him into her empty, waiting pussy.

He gave only one more hard thrust forward, knocking her thighs into the pool table with bruising force. Nell bit down on her lip to keep from crying out when he backed away.

"Now." He tapped her ass with the hard tip of the riding crop again, then did the same to Gemma beside her. "Let's begin."

Alternating back and forth, Mason peppered both of their bottoms with strokes from the crop, spreading them around with obvious care. By the time he took a break, Nell was confident her entire ass glowed a rosy pink—but also felt almost sure he hadn't even touched the stripes from the cane. That would've hurt a hell of a lot more.

She didn't have much time to marvel at his precision, though. Not when Mason almost immediately said, "I think that'll do for a warm-up."

Most Doms would say that in one of two ways—either in a voice positively dripping with lust and shared excitement, or in that hard Dom voice generally reserved for real punishments.

Mason St. John clearly wasn't most Doms. The words came out cold and calculated, as though he was doing the math in his head to determine exactly how many strokes each of his slaves needed, and with exactly how much force to teach them the proper lesson. It sent a whole new kind of shiver running down Nell's spine.

"Count your strokes aloud," Mason ordered, still using the calculating tone that both confused and excited her. "If you miscount in any way, we start over, do I make myself clear?"

"Yes, Master." Nell and Gemma said it in near-perfect unison.

"Very well. Time to continue."

Everything that happened after that was absolute fucking chaos. The strokes rained down with incredible speed, faster than they could get the numbers out. Sometimes, the slapper hit in a way that left her skin hot and tingly, sending a line of pleasure straight to her clit, making her nipples ache. Other times, a stroke fell with such force it temporarily stole the breath from her lungs, forcing her to gasp out the number as best she could.

Three strokes to Nell, one to Gemma, two to Nell, five to Gemma, ten straight to Nell, four particularly harsh strokes to Gemma that left her sobbing. On and on it went like that, without any discernible pattern whatsoever. She was so uncertain, so terrified of what would come next, she tensed every single muscle in her body like she was a sprinter waiting for the starting gun.

Twice, the count had to start over. First, when Mason followed the line of a raised cane welt with lightning-fast strokes, all she could do was scream. The second time, Gemma got mixed up and called out Nell's number instead.

The motherfucker was confusing them on purpose, and Nell sagged against the pool table as she cried, trying with a wild desperation to concentrate on the count as he systematically flayed her body and mind apart.

Nell felt like she was drifting away, almost like an out of body experience, when Mason finally stilled. This wasn't subspace—it was something else entirely.

Gemma's unbound hand slid across the distance between them, finding Nell's. Fingers lacing together, Nell held onto the other woman like a lifeline, using that connection to ground her back in her body.

The leather slapper slid slowly around the circumference of their linked hands, with a gentleness that shocked Nell. She expected him to use the crop to force them apart.

"I see." Mason's tone gave nothing away as he continued to circle their hands with the end of the riding crop. "Perhaps I was mistaken. Perhaps this wasn't a case of naughty, impatient little girls who couldn't keep their hands to themselves."

Well . . . it kind of was at first if she was being honest. Gemma was stunningly beautiful, seductive in a way she didn't know how to refuse, and Nell had longed to kiss and touch her. Far be it from her to refuse Gemma's invitation to do just that.

But Nell wasn't an idiot. She chose not to say any of that out loud.

"Since you two have obviously formed a genuine attachment to one another, it would be cruel keep you apart." Taking hold of both women by the hair, he hauled them up into standing positions. With the absolute inferno of throbbing pain that made up her ass and upper thighs, Nell could spare little more than a wince for the rough handling.

Mason led them toward the card tables, kicking out a straight back chair and pushing Gemma down onto it. She shrieked as her abused bottom hit the seat, and a new batch of tears shone in her green eyes. Marching Nell around in front of the chair, he unhooked her cuffs from the garter harness one at a time, then pushed her down to her knees between Gemma's spread thighs.

"Stay." Mason looked them both in the eye, ensuring neither could claim they thought they weren't included in the command.

As Mason stalked over to a credenza along the back wall, digging around behind its four identical doors, Gemma and Nell stared at one another. Too afraid to speak, they said everything they could with their eyes instead.

I'm sorry I got you in so much trouble.

I'd do it all over again if I had the choice.

So would I.

It means everything to me that I'm not alone.

How different her life with Micah might have been if Gemma—or anyone else—had been there with her. She wouldn't have shrunk into herself for so long. Maybe, just maybe, she would've found the strength to leave him sooner.

Years sooner.

Warmth flashed through her chest as she thought about her conversation with Holly that morning. About Mistress Freya, setting this whole thing up out of the kindness of her heart. About Rafe, the Manor's Official Scary Dom, not only easing Nell back into the lifestyle, but easing her back into *life*.

She wasn't alone anymore. And she'd never let herself be alone again.

When Mason returned, a bundle of nylon rope dangled from one fist. Crouching down behind the chair, he tugged Gemma's wrists together behind her back, tying them with an intricate knot. Two loops of rope extended from the sides of the knot, looking almost like wings.

While Nell tried to puzzle out what those were for, Mason held out both his hands, palms up. "Give me your hands."

She pressed her palms against his in two seconds flat. The last thing she wanted from him was another punishment.

Yanking her forward until her ribs practically hit the front of the chair, he attached her cuffs to the two loops of rope. "Pull as hard as you can," he ordered. "Make sure it's secure." It took only seconds to prove the man knew his way around a length of rope.

"Now." Mason drew out the word as he slowly stood. "I believe I've waited long enough to take my pleasure." Reaching down, he gripped Nell's chin, forcing her to look up at him. Eyes boring into hers, freezing her in place, he said, "Whether or not you two join me is entirely up to you."

"What do you want me to do, Master?" She barely got the words past the lump in her throat.

Mason moved his thumb along her cheek in a single, gentle stroke. "I'm going to fuck you. Hard. While I do, you will attempt to make Gemma come with only your tongue." Gemma's thighs jerked, squeezing around Nell's shoulders. "If you succeed, you get to come, too. If not?" He shrugged. "There's always tomorrow."

Oh, challenge absolutely fucking accepted, asshole.

As Mason slipped around behind her, Nell got right to work. Burying her face between the other woman's thighs, she lapped at Gemma's pussy with her tongue, then slid up the full length of her slit. Rolling her tongue over and around Gemma's clit, she returned to her pussy and started all over again.

Nell half moaned, half shrieked as Mason dug his fingers into her hips, lifting her ass into the air. "Good girl," he murmured, pushing two fingers into her dripping pussy. He pumped them in and out of her, taking his time, spreading and twisting his fingers to explore her pulsing inner walls.

Fucking hell, this would be harder than she anticipated. His fingers felt *so. Fucking. Good.* It was already a struggle to concentrate, and he hadn't even started fucking her yet.

Lick, goddamn you! She shouted it inside her own mind as she redoubled her efforts, flattening her tongue against Gemma's clit, giving the bundle of nerves some serious pressure. Her reward was a moan that sent heat coursing through her veins.

She had just started to swirl her tongue at the entrance of Gemma's pussy when Mason slammed into her from behind. Thank Christ her mouth was occupied, or she definitely would've earned herself another punishment for bad language.

Mason pounded into her again and again, each stroke punctuated by the slap of his hips against her punished ass. The stretch and the burn felt exquisite. This was her favorite feeling in the entire world—a long, hard fucking while a recent punishment still scorched her skin. Closing her eyes, she lost herself in the sensations.

"Nell, *hurry*."

Gemma's plea was like a slap to the face, snapping her back to the present moment. Fucking hell, she couldn't let herself get distracted, or neither of them would be allowed to come.

Ignoring Gemma's pussy entirely, she focused all her efforts on the blonde's clit. Twisting, laving, sucking, biting. She used the jerks and quivering of Gemma's thighs against her face to judge how everything affected her—to push her higher and higher without reprieve.

"Oh my God, oh my God!" Gemma shouted the words over and over, her head thrown back, the muscles of her inner thighs hard as stone against Nell's face.

And then it happened at last. A shudder ripped through Gemma's body as she screamed.

Yanking Nell's head out of the way, Mason used his other hand to plunge two fingers into Gemma's pussy, leaving them there as the woman's inner walls spasmed. It wasn't until Gemma slumped in the chair, utterly spent, that Mason withdrew his now-glistening fingers.

"Good girl." Mason whispered the words into Nell's ear as he undid the Velcro on her cuffs, freeing her at last.

Holding her back against his chest, his hard strokes didn't even falter as he reached down to find her clit, his fingers slick as they rubbed. Knowing it was Gemma's moisture and not her own made Nell throw her head back against Mason's shoulder and moan.

God, this was so fucked up. So overwhelmingly erotic. So perfect.

When Mason's careful rhythm finally grew more erratic, Nell closed her eyes, trying to lose herself in every single feeling coursing through her body. His cock, hard as iron as it slammed into her. The sweet taste of Gemma lingering on her tongue. The new eruption of fire across her punished skin with each stroke. The slide of his fingers over her clit, circling faster, faster, faster. Even the light scratch of his sparse chest hair against her back.

It was too much. Way too fucking much. Her pleasure erupted from her center like a volcano, the heat tearing through her, destroying her, leaving behind nothing but a burnt, empty husk.

Nell had no idea how long she'd been out of it. Since post-coital comas probably weren't a thing, subspace seemed the most likely culprit of her current confusion.

Blinking, she tried to get her eyes to focus in the too-bright room. "Rafe? Where's Rafe?"

Rafe's gray-green eyes and dark beard swam into focus above her. "Right here, kitten." Everything was so gentle. Eyes. Voice. Lips that almost formed a smile.

Could hair be gentle? He looked like he had gentle hair.

And what a weird fucking thought that was.

"No," she said, shaking her head. Jesus, why was her head so fuzzy? Nothing made any sense. "You're not gentle. You're the scary one."

Though his brows arched, he seemed amused, not angry. *Gentle amusement.*

Goddamn it, why was he being so fucking nice to her? Was her life so fucked up that even Rafe Erikson—the Dom the naughtiest of Manor guests got sent to when their own Doms couldn't punish them hard enough—was treating her like a fragile little bird with a broken wing?

"Come on," he whispered, scooping her up off the floor. "Let's put you to bed."

She didn't want to be carried to bed and tucked in with care. She wanted Rafe to throw her over his shoulder, carry her down to the dungeon, and cane her until she couldn't even see straight anymore. Then he could fuck her into oblivion, taking his own pleasure again and again, paying no attention to hers.

Christ, the very idea had her pussy pulsing again.

But as she snuggled her face against the soft fabric of his T-shirt, breathing in the scents of cedar and leather, wood polish and burning leaves, the crude fantasy drifted away.

Both, a Holly-ish voice in her head said. *Both is better.*

After all, she hadn't wanted both with Micah, and look where that got her.

As her eyes fluttered closed, she thought perhaps the existence of one end of the spectrum was what made the other end so exquisite.

CHAPTER 12

Rafe

Global warming definitely sucked balls. But it was really hard not to enjoy it when northern Vermont was in the mid-seventies the day before Halloween.

Rafe had come out of the shower to Nell curled up in a chair by an open window, a dreamy look on her face. Since his sweet, mischievous little sub's body could use a break after the last few days, he decided then and there that some fresh air would do them both good.

And apparently they weren't the only ones. They found Aiden and Olivia on the front porch, curled up together on a loveseat, her head in his lap. It hadn't taken much to convince the pair to join them on the front lawn. Especially after Rafe gave his fellow Dom a loaded look over Nell's head.

Nell and Olivia had the potential to be great friends if given enough of an opportunity. If Rafe had ever been a hundred percent sure of anything in his life, he was sure of that. They were kindred spirits—both kinder and more cheerful than people with their pasts had any right to be, as far as he was concerned. And both women had found a strength he couldn't even fathom, learning how to trust and submit after everything that happened to them.

Knowing how much good Olivia could do for his new little sub's healing process, he wasn't about to pass up the chance.

When Luca arrived with a picnic basket and a second blanket a few minutes later ("Compliments of Zach," he said when greeted by four surprised looks), it truly felt like a perfect morning.

The muffins and mimosas long since gone, the party split. Rafe and Aiden stayed on the original blanket, while the girls moved about ten feet away. Sprawled out on the second blanket in their lingerie, they soaked in the unseasonable sun while they whispered and giggled like a couple of teenagers.

For the life of him, Rafe couldn't figure out why he found the sight so ridiculously appealing.

It wasn't simply that he enjoyed their bodies, though that much was definitely true. He'd scened with Olivia a handful of times in the last ten or so months, and loved her curves almost as much as he adored Nell's long, lithe body. The pair of them together deserved to have artists painting them, poets writing sonnets, and all that sappy renaissance shit.

And it wasn't only the self-satisfied feeling of knowing how very right he'd been about Nell and Olivia forming a genuine friendship. The more friends Nell had in her life—especially those involved in the lifestyle themselves—the better.

He watched the pair for several more seconds, smiling to himself as he tried to work it out. When it finally hit him, his mouth dropped open for a moment. He snapped it closed again, hoping no one noticed.

As the morning warmed up, the girls had taken off most of their clothes, even slipping off their bra straps to avoid tan lines. It seemed sexy and fun while they stripped, and he and Aiden enjoyed the way the girls preened and arched their backs, throwing covert looks their way from time to time.

But it only just occurred to him that every single one of Nell's scars was visible. Including the half-carved name on her hip. Even a few days ago, Nell balked at the idea of him seeing the scars.

Yet here she was, mostly naked in front of two near-strangers, not a hint of shame on her radiant face, her hands never once creeping in to cover the thick, raised lines.

Jesus fucking Christ, she was incredible. He'd never met a woman like her in his entire life, and he couldn't imagine he ever would again.

"They certainly seem to be getting along," Aiden said.

Rafe glanced over to find Aiden leaning back on his hands, a speculative look in his eyes. But it wasn't directed at their subs. It was directed at him.

"Why are you looking at me like that?" Rafe demanded, scowling. People kept giving him the weirdest looks, but no one would explain why. It was fucking annoying.

Aiden's smug half smile did *not* help matters. "If you have to ask, you're not ready to hear the answer."

Rafe growled. He couldn't help himself. "Fair warning, jackass, if you're going to act like a fortune cookie, I'm going to treat you like one."

"Meaning what?" Aiden actually had the audacity to chuckle, the fucker. "You'll break me in half and rip out my insides?"

Rafe's answering smile was anything but friendly. "Something along those lines, yeah." But his phone buzzed in his pocket before he had a chance to follow through on the threat.

Giving his friend a *this-isn't-over-asshole* look, he dug out his phone and glanced down at the screen. The call was coming from Seattle, Washington.

"Nell, I think it's for you," Rafe said, tossing his phone onto the blanket beside her.

Her hands shook as she picked it up. For a second, he thought she would let it go to voicemail. But then she drew in a deep breath, mumbled, "Fuck it," and slid a fingertip along the bottom of the screen. Even so, her brown irises were lost in a pool of white as she brought the phone up to her ear. "Hello?"

Two voices screamed on the other end, so loud that Nell yanked the phone away from her ear. Even Olivia leaned away, scrunching up her nose at the sound.

Rafe had a hard time following exactly how it went down after that. Nell screamed too, then cried, and then she was screaming *and* crying, rolling around on the blanket with her legs kicking up like an excited puppy.

Words came out of her a mile a minute, but it was so disjointed and confusing, he couldn't follow the conversation at all. As if the people on the other end kept finishing her sentences, and she kept completing theirs.

After a few minutes of this, during which the other three watched her with varying levels of bemusement, she looked over at Rafe with joy radiating out of her like literal fucking sunshine. "It's Ben and Cady," she mouthed, pointing to the phone, smiling like her greatest dream just came true.

Then she was up, pacing back and forth across the enormous front lawn, nothing but hints of her animated voice drifting over to him.

"I'm dying to know what that's all about," Olivia said, scurrying over to their blanket and settling between Aiden's sprawled legs.

Aiden kissed the top of her head before saying, "That makes two of us."

It took Rafe a few seconds to figure out how much of her story he had any right to tell. "The short version is, she got away from her major piece of shit ex a little over a year ago. The guy fucked up her relationships with her friends and family, and I'm helping her get back in touch with everyone. She talked to her sister yesterday, and those are her two best friends on the phone."

"And the long version?" Aiden prompted, his voice carefully neutral. Olivia blinked back tears.

"You'll have to ask her about that."

Brows drawing together in concern, Aiden watched Nell pace for several long seconds. "The scars?"

"Like I said, her ex was a major piece of shit."

"Christ. If I'd known that, I would've bid more in the auction yesterday." Aiden drew his lips into a tight line. "No wonder you asked if she could keep the money."

Olivia's hands balled into fists somewhere along the line. He had no doubt that if Micah strolled across the lawn at that moment, she'd beat the ever-loving shit out of him without a second thought.

Yeah, well. She'd have to get in fucking line.

"She was terrified of me seeing her scars on her first day. Now look at her." His chest swelled with pride. His strong, beautiful badass.

"Can I ask you a question?"

Rafe narrowed his eyes at Olivia. She sounded a tad too intention-ally sweet and innocent. "Your tone tells me I'm going to regret this, but go ahead."

"Do you like Nell?"

"Liv—" Aiden started in a warning tone.

But Rafe talked right over him, his brows shooting up. "Like her? Of course I like her. What's not to like?"

"No, no, no." Ignoring her own Dom's tight grip on her upper arm, she waved a dismissive hand in Rafe's direction. "I mean, do you *like* Nell. Do you have feelings for her."

If she sucker punched him in the gut, it would've surprised him less. Hell, the world could've erupted into nuclear war, and he might have taken it with more grace.

At least everything finally made sense. All the funny looks, the bizarre-ass comments . . . everyone thought he'd gone soft. That a woman had finally come along who could cage and tame the beast.

But not one of them ever bothered to find out why he became a beast in the first place.

"She's a guest. She's leaving in three days so my next guest can come. End of fucking discussion." No longer able to look at his friends, Rafe stood, stomping off across the yard in the opposite direction from Nell. Last thing he wanted was for her to see his face and end her call early. Not during the big reunion with her friends. He couldn't take that away from her.

But seriously, what the fuck kind of a question was that? Did he *like* Nell? Absolutely fucking preposterous.

So what if Aiden and Olivia found their so-called eternal bliss with one another? That didn't give Olivia the right to meddle in other people's lives, stirring up shit that needed to stay fucking buried.

Of course he fucking had feelings for Nell. What a stupid fucking question. The question Olivia hadn't asked—the one that actually mattered—was a different thing entirely.

Did he plan to do anything about those feelings?

And there was only one possible answer he'd ever be able to give—a great, big, resounding *no fucking way.*

He already had his heart ripped out of his chest once. Though it wasn't visible, the hole was still there—a great, gaping wound, jagged and empty. Rafe could feel it every day when he woke, every night while he tried to fall asleep.

Some wounds scar over or fade with time. Others . . . others are forever.

And those are the kinds of injuries you can't survive more than once.

"Rafe?"

He jerked away from the hand on his shoulder, leaping off the garden bench before he recognized Nell's voice. "Shit, I'm sorry," he said, moving around the bench to gather her to his chest.

She was stiff in his arms, and several awkward seconds passed before she asked, "Did I do something wrong, Sir?" in a small, timid voice.

"No." He held her even closer, breathing a sigh of relief when she finally relaxed against him. "I'm sorry. I know I've been on edge all day."

That was putting it mildly. He ignored her while she researched potential master's degree programs after their picnic, scrolling angrily through his phone the whole time. When she proudly showed him a list of colleges, complete with pros and cons for each one, he hardly even glanced at it.

The hurt in her eyes felt good at the time. Maybe that's what they both needed—to hurt each other before they got too deep into their stupid fucking feelings.

He did feel bad when she decided not to complete any more tasks, though. It was obvious she was too upset after the way he was acting to lose herself in a fantasy anyway, so what was the point?

Unfortunately, that guilty pit in his stomach only pissed him off even more, and he said things he absolutely didn't mean. "Well, then." He'd heard the cruelty in his own voice, loving and hating it at the same time. "If you're sick of fucking me, I wish you'd go ahead and say so. I'm not standing in your way if you'd rather go find someone else."

With that, he'd stalked out of the room without a backward glance, pretending he couldn't hear her cry.

That had been hours ago. The sun almost finished setting by the time she found him sulking on the garden bench.

Fucking hell, he was so ashamed.

Pushing Nell out to arm's length, he waited until she looked up into his eyes on her own. "I'm sorry. I know I fucked everything up today." With a deep, steeling breath, he forced himself to add, "If you're willing to go on a walk with me, I'll explain why. But I'll understand completely if you don't want me unloading my shit on you. No hard feelings either way."

The worry and pain in her brown eyes seemed to melt away, replaced by so much kindness it made his chest hurt. How this beautiful creature walked through fire for over a decade without letting it burn away all the goodness inside of her was beyond comprehension.

"Come on," he said, taking her hand, leading her deeper into the extensive, manicured garden. Most of the summer flowers had withered away, but the Manor's landscaping crew made sure the enormous garden always looked its best, no matter the season. He focused on the mums and goldenrod, the asters and witch hazel as they walked between the low square hedges. He made it all the way to the gate separating the garden from the pool before he managed to speak. "Olivia said something to me today, and it reminded me of—well, not reminded really, but it got me thinking about—*fuck*."

Christ almighty, where to begin? The only person he'd ever talked to about any of this was Freya, and she knew all the pertinent details already. He never had to figure out the perfect place to start, the best way to relay so much fucked up information so it all made sense.

"Would it help if I put you over my knee while I ask you questions and spank you when you don't answer?" Nell asked in a mock-angelic tone.

The worst of the tension in his chest eased away as he laughed. "No, I don't think it would." He leaned his forearms along the top of the gate. "I appreciate the thought, though."

She bumped her shoulder against his. "Anytime."

Perfection was nothing but a pipe dream. Time to make himself start talking and hope for the best. "You remember when we met, and I told you I only ever let women I've collared call me Master?"

"Of course."

"The truth is, I've only ever collared one woman. It was"—he did some quick math in his head—"eighteen years ago. Fuck, I'm getting old." He ran his free hand through his hair. "Anyway. We met at a club down in Tampa."

Surprise filled her eyes as she looked up at him. "You lived in Tampa, too?"

"For a while. I moved around a lot after high school. My parents wanted me to go into the Army like my dad and grandpa and great grandpa, back and back and back." He stared out over the pool, watching the bright blue water ripple in the breeze. With the weather as warm as it had been, and the pool being heated, they hadn't bothered closing it for the season yet. He sighed. "I wanted to make them proud, but I knew it wasn't for me. I'd known since I was a little kid."

Nell looked over with sympathy in her eyes. "That must've been really tough."

"It was what it was," he said, shrugging. "I knew from the get-go they wouldn't pay for college or even sign the student loan forms unless I served at least four years, and I didn't have the grades for a scholarship. So I didn't even try. I graduated, found a job and a cheap apartment in a different state, and accepted my fate as their greatest disappointment."

That made her tense up beside him, and he regretted his word choice immediately. So wrapped up in his own shit, he forgot for a second that her parents disowned her. At least he still spoke to his mom and dad. He was just the black sheep among his career military brother and Westpoint graduate sister.

"After a few years, I got a job doing parasailing tours down in Tampa. The pay was shit but the tips were unreal. Easiest job I ever had in my life." He drove tourists around the bay seven days a week, then partied at clubs or on the beach almost every night. He'd felt energized, invincible, utterly alive—like his life was fucking perfect.

It was the last time he could remember being truly happy.

"Some friends dragged me to a new club one night," he said, forcing himself to keep telling the story and not get lost in his head. "I'd never even heard of it, and I assumed it was like all the other places we went. A dance club or a bar—the kind of place we could meet pretty girls."

When he didn't continue right away, she asked, "Was it a BDSM club?"

Rafe nodded, remembering the red lights, the smell of leather, the music so loud your partner had to scream their safeword for you to hear it. "I felt things that night I didn't even have the words to describe. The other guys were there as a joke, for a good story. But something in me awakened that night. When they got bored and left, I stayed. I wanted to learn everything I could."

"And that's where you met her. The woman you collared."

"Yes." He closed his eyes, remembering her short bushy hair, her lips pressing together into a heart shape when she smiled, and the come-hither stare she gave him from across the club. With a sigh, he forced his eyes to open. "Her name was Jessica."

There was genuine strain in Nell's voice when she forced out, "Did you fall in love with her?"

"Yes." There was no point in sugarcoating it. Not if she had any chance of understanding. "We were both twenty-one. Young, stupid, always looking for the next exciting thing. For a while, we found everything we wanted in each other. When she accepted my collar, I thought we'd be happy forever. It all seemed so perfect."

He'd been entranced by Jess—by her willingness to submit to any whim that crossed his mind. The parties and barhopping with the guys stopped basically overnight; from their first meeting on, whenever they weren't at work, they were together.

"What happened?" She still sounded uncomfortable, but there was a softness to it now. Like she knew this story would have a terrible end.

"After a while, she wanted more from me." He winced as he remembered the first time Jess brought it up. The screaming match that followed. "She wanted to go harder. Deeper. *Darker.*"

The blush heating Nell's entire face could've started a wildfire during a drought. The poor thing. She'd done exactly the same thing to her ex Brian, ending up in Micah's clutches as a result. He could only imagine what she felt right now.

Hoping to get through it as quickly as possible, to put them both out of their misery, he kept going. "She wanted to try things I knew absolutely nothing about—things that weren't safe for total amateurs to try without some training. Things like extended suspension. Fire play." He had to force the last part out through clenched teeth. "Breath play."

Christ, her eyes were so wide. "Did you do them anyway?"

"No." He looked away, biting at the inside of his cheek as he tried to figure out what to say next. "I talked to some other tops at the club, looking for someone to mentor me. That's where I met Freya. I started working with her to learn as much as I could. I told Jess if she could wait, I'd learn *anything* for her. But I wasn't going to risk hurting her."

"What happened?" Nell asked again, voice shaking.

"She called me a pussy and said she'd find a real man who wasn't afraid to give her what she wanted." That came out much harsher than he intended. He hadn't realized he was still mad about it after all these years. Though he supposed that's what happened when you repressed your feelings instead of dealing with them. "And that's more or less what she did. She found someone dumber than me willing to do anything she wanted—dangerous fucking experiments with someone else's life on the line."

"*Oh my God.*" She slapped her hand over her mouth and stared up at him, hardly even breathing.

With a harsh, humorless laugh, he said, "I guess you figured out the ending."

Nell continued to stare at him, hand over her mouth, words completely failing her.

"Police ruled it an accident. And I have no reason to believe otherwise. The guy called 911 himself when he realized she didn't start breathing again." He sounded like a fucking robot. Like he was reading a news story about a total stranger, not talking about his own life. "He performed CPR while he waited for the ambulance. Even offered to help pay for her funeral, though her family wanted nothing to do with him."

Tears sparkled in her eyes. "I'm so, so sorry."

Rafe swallowed down the lump in his throat. "Her family didn't want me at the funeral either. They knew exactly who I was. We were together for over a year, and she'd told her sister all about me. When I tried to talk to her parents, they called me a freak. Said I tricked their daughter into going down the path that led to her death. That it was my fault."

"No." She reached up to cup his face, only remembering his rules when he jerked away. Hurt flashed through her eyes as she forced her hands down to her sides. "Rafe, that's not even close to true. You met her at a kink club, for fuck's sake. She was the one trying to lead *you* down the path."

Closing his eyes, he imagined how soft Nell's hands would feel against his face. How her warmth would seep into his skin. "I know." All he could do was whisper. "But I kept telling myself if I'd just given in, she'd still be alive. I would've been more careful than him. I would've stopped sooner. She was dead because I was too afraid to even try."

"*No,*" she said again, with more force this time. "That's not even a little bit true. Please tell me you don't still think that."

"Not all the time."

Her hands twitched, as if she longed to reach for him again. "Can I hug you?" she asked, leaning away slightly as if she expected him to lash out. "Please?"

Voice failing him completely, all he could do was nod.

Nell moved her hands to his chest, then wrapped her arms around his middle, holding him close. Face buried in his neck, she whispered, "You shouldn't ever have to think it again. You made the right choice. The only safe choice. You have no idea what she would've pushed you to do if you went along with it. It just as easily could've been you who killed her."

Tears welled behind his closed eyes as he tried to breathe. Fucking hell, why couldn't he breathe? This was why he never talked about any of this. It hurt too fucking much.

"It's okay. You don't have to keep it all inside anymore. It's better to let it out." She was still whispering, her lips only inches from his ear. Her voice was so fucking sweet. It almost made him want to believe her.

Swallowing down the sob trapped in his throat by sheer force of will, Rafe said, "I completely fell apart after the funeral. Went on a bender that lasted for weeks. Got fired from my job. Missed a rent payment and was about to get evicted. Then one night, after a bottle of Jack . . ." He shuddered.

"It's okay," she whispered again. "I promise it's okay."

Maybe it actually would be. Maybe it was finally time to let it all go.

Rafe extracted himself from her arms with gentle care, not wanting to startle or upset her, then took her hand in his. Bringing it up to the inside of his wrist, he traced the tip of her forefinger down a short, thin scar concealed by the eagle tattoo wrapping around his forearm, its wings spread wide.

Nell gasped, tears springing to her eyes again. "Oh, Rafe."

"I didn't get far before I came to my senses. I called Freya, and she got to my place so fast, she must've run a hundred red lights to do it. She patched me up and took me to live with her and Ian."

One corner of her lips lifted into a wobbly smile. "So she saved us both."

"She helped us both," he corrected. "As for saving? I don't know. I'm the one who called her. You're the one who left Micah. We had to do the actual saving parts on our own."

New tears started their long, slow tracks down her cheeks.

"After Freya and Ian got me to stop drinking, I started volunteering as a dungeon monitor at the club. I studied the scenes, learning as much as I could. Freya got some of her friends who liked to play harder than she does to mentor me, too." He pulled Nell against him, needing to feel her heat before he could make himself say any more. "I spent three years in Tampa before I mastered everything I could there. Then I moved to New Orleans, then Baltimore, then Chicago. Everywhere I went, I found people who could teach me something new, and worked my ass off until I was certain any sub would be safe in my hands, no matter what she needed."

Nell's hands fisted in his shirt. "That's why you came here. So you'd be famous in our circles." She stumbled through the words, clearly on the edge of more tears. "It's why you let everyone think you're scary."

He kissed the top of her head and held her even closer.

"So girls like me will go to you, and you can keep us safe."

"I didn't know what else to do." Christ, he sounded so lost. "And somewhere along the line, I think I kind of forgot it started out as an act. I don't know which parts are really me anymore."

Clinging to him, Nell finally gave in to her tears. And for the first time in almost two decades, Rafe did the same.

CHAPTER 13

Nell

W hen Nell woke the next morning, Rafe's soft snores drifted over from the other side of the king bed. She rolled over a few times, trying to find a comfortable position, but ultimately gave up. Her body made it abundantly clear it was time to get up.

Not surprising, really. Rafe needed to let off some steam last night, and she'd gladly obliged. Wearing nothing but black leather pants that made him look like a sex god, he handcuffed her naked to a chain dangling from the dungeon ceiling. Then he used a bullwhip on every single inch of sensitive skin on her body.

Each fall of the whip felt like a line of icy fire, making her scream and writhe. And yet the whip didn't break the skin. Not once. The skill with which he wielded it left her astounded even now, hours later.

Then he wrapped the braided leather around her throat, using it to cut off her air as he fucked her well into the night, only letting her gasp in enough labored breaths to stay conscious. As if he needed to prove to himself he could do it. That no matter what he did, he could keep her safe.

She didn't even know how many times she came last night. She lost count somewhere along the way.

What she did know was she'd need a vacation to recover from her vacation. Even Micah didn't have the stamina or all-consuming desire to use her so fully.

Tiptoeing around the suite, she did the absolute minimum of her morning routine in the bathroom, slipped on a pair of sweats and a tank top, and padded out to the hall. Once she safely closed the door behind her, she relaxed, heading downstairs in search of caffeine. She was halfway down the curved staircase when she noticed Zach behind the reception desk.

Zach smiled broadly as soon as their gazes met. "Good morning, Nell."

"Good morning." The caffeine could wait. She crossed the lobby quickly, the marble tiles smooth and cool beneath her bare feet. "I wanted to thank you for our little picnic yesterday. That was so sweet."

His smile finally reached his eyes. "My pleasure. I'm glad you all enjoyed yourselves." Glancing toward the empty staircase, he asked, "Is your handsome prince still asleep?"

She laughed as she pictured him dressed up like the prince in *Sleeping Beauty*. "For now."

"Then let me be the first to wish you a happy Halloween," Zach said with another big grin.

"Happy Halloween," she said back, leaning against the reception counter. "I *love* your bow tie." It was covered in little grinning jack-o-lanterns.

Zach's lips got all sorts of wobbly, and he put a hand over his heart. "Thank you." He wiped a fake tear from the corner of one eye. "I've been wearing themed bow ties for every single holiday for *literally years*. And you're the first person in this place to ever say a thing about it. Which I'm pretty sure means we're now best friends."

Nell's laugh rang through the lobby, echoing back from the vaulted ceiling. "Oh, is that how it works? Good to know, bestie. Speaking of, I'm surprised there aren't any decorations around here." She took a glance around, though she already knew she wouldn't find anything.

He heaved a dramatic sigh. "I ask about decorations every year, but no one around here seems to care. Which, if you think about it, makes absolutely no sense. Every single person in this place is kinky as fuck."

"Right? We're literally a group of people *obsessed* with sexy little costumes. Halloween was made for us."

Light straight-up glittered in Zach's bright eyes. "Okay, joking aside, I think we can claim the besties title now."

Nell was pretty sure he was still joking. That didn't stop his declaration from warming her heart. It was like that lovely, weird feeling she got after taking a big gulp of hot chocolate, like tendrils spreading out from the center of her chest. "What do you say we rebel?"

At that, his smile turned downright impish. "Explain."

"Let's throw the first annual Fairford Manor Halloween party," she said, her mind moving at lightspeed as she formulated a whole plan. "Send out official invites and everything. What are they gonna do, not attend their own party?"

Zach's whole face lit up like a kid on Christmas morning. "You are *diabolical*." Grabbing her hand, he led her around the edge of the desk and into his little office.

An antique wooden desk took up nearly one whole wall, the top strewn with several stacks of papers and files, an open laptop off to one side.

Dropping into the fancy-ass burgundy leather desk chair, Zach swiped his thumb across the touchpad. A login screen appeared asking for his pin.

042988.

She didn't mean to follow his fingers as they typed in the password. It just sort of . . . happened.

A long, complicated spreadsheet with what looked to be hundreds of rows and columns filled the screen. She didn't get more than a glance at it before Zach minimized the window. As he pulled up an internet browser, she glanced around the rest of the small office.

Aside from the framed art on the walls and a few potted plants, the only other thing here was a long, narrow table with an office-style mailbox on top. It was split into multiple labeled cubbyholes, most of the cubbies empty or nearly so. The one labeled *Aiden*, on the other hand, overflowed onto the table beneath.

"Okay then," Zach said, rubbing his hands together as the screen filled with Halloween party decorations. "There's no way we can get anything delivered same-day all the way up here. But planning our party for tomorrow gives people enough time to come up with costumes anyway. Let's see what we can get here with overnight shipping."

Nell leaned over his shoulder as they scrolled through pages and pages of potential decorations, ranging from spooky to silly, grotesque to elegant. Basically anything they both liked ended up in the cart, though they realized they'd have to rein it in quite a bit when they saw the total.

"Yeah, if I spend over two grand on sparkly pumpkins, I might not have a job tomorrow," Zach said with a laugh. "I'm gonna run to the bathroom really quick. You start narrowing this down." He scurried off, the soles of his shoes clicking against the lobby's marble tiles.

As Nell sat down, she had every intention of doing as he asked. And yet, she found herself opening a new tab.

No. The admonishment in her head was definitely in Holly's bossy voice.

And not-Holly was right. She'd gone more than twenty-four hours without giving into the urge to check her old email. Noelle Eliza Beaumont had her goddamn closure, and there was nothing more to be said or done.

"Oh, fuck me," she muttered as she pulled up the page and signed in.

The newest email from Micah had arrived at 1:02 that morning.

Muttering, "You're a fucking moron," under her breath, she clicked on it. It was a hell of a lot shorter than the last one. Holding her breath, she read.

Dearest Noelle,

I'm sorry to learn you're not ready to reply to me, though I promise I don't blame you. Not one bit. I know how much I hurt you. I can't even imagine how long it'll take to heal from so much pain.

I just want you to know that I love you. You're the only woman I'll ever love. And I'm willing to wait, however long it takes.

Love,

Micah

She pushed all the trapped air out of her lungs, closing her eyes. Why the fuck did she read that? What exactly was she trying to achieve here?

He broke her, then literally carved up the pieces. Why in the fucking fuck was she allowing even the tiniest, darkest, most fucked-up part of her brain feel guilty that he sounded sad?

Aww, poor little psycho, so sad he lost his favorite toy.

Oh yeah, Nell definitely liked that part of her brain better.

The hard soles of Zach's shiny dress shoes rang out against the tile once more. Heart leaping up into her throat, Nell hurried to sign out, then remove her account from the list of possible sign-ins. She only just closed the tab when he strolled in, leaning down to examine their shopping cart.

Zach looked down his nose at her, smirking. "I see Operation Narrow Down the Cart was a huge success."

"I tried," she said, drawing out the second word, doing her best to sound remorseful. "But I don't work here. It made me nervous making such a big decision for the Manor."

"Oh, all right," he said, throwing up his hands in mock-defeat. "I'll do it. Up you get."

Rafe found them huddled together half an hour later, still working to narrow it all down. "There you are," he said, moving up behind her, running a warm hand down her arm. "I've been looking everywhere for you."

She turned, going up on her toes so he could give her a good morning kiss. His tongue tasted like fresh toothpaste, making her glad she at least did a cursory brush before sneaking out of the suite.

"And what are you two up to in here?" Rafe asked when they finally broke apart.

"Nothing," they said in perfect unison. Neither of them sounded remotely truthful.

One corner of Rafe's mouth twitched. "Looks like someone wants an early morning spanking today."

Throwing a flirty glance over his shoulder, Zach quipped, "I mean, if you're offering."

Rafe rolled his eyes. "You wish, pretty boy." He tried to get a look at the laptop screen, but Zach had already minimized the window. "All right, all right. Keep your secrets. But at least one of you is going to pay for them." Grabbing Nell's hand, he pulled her from the room. Zach watched them go with a wide grin.

She trotted along in his wake as they crossed the lobby. But when he walked right past the stairs, Nell asked, "Sir, may I please go upstairs and get dressed?"

Rafe stopped only long enough to glance over his shoulder. "You look fine to me. Come on."

She'd brushed her teeth and put on fresh deodorant, so it wasn't a worst-case scenario, but there was no way she looked *fine*. The sweatpants may have been new and clean, without the holes and stains of some of her other pairs. But they were still baggy and ugly, and not at all the sort of thing she'd been wearing so far that week. They were only supposed to be for downtime, not sexy times.

Without any other options, Nell followed her Dom down the hallway to the parlor. The moment he passed through the doorway, Rafe said, "Get undressed and into position," without even glancing back at her.

She froze on the threshold, worrying at her bottom lip with her teeth. He already told her not to go upstairs, but maybe, if he actually understood—

"*Nell.*"

She started guiltily at the reprimand in his voice. "But Sir, I—"

"Just do as I say," he interrupted, dropping down onto the sofa, half sprawled on the blue cushions. "It wasn't exactly a complicated request."

Ice ran through Nell's veins. Closing her eyes, she focused on the electric tingling in her fingertips, counting out her heartbeats until she felt calm again.

Only then did she realize she was, once again, not following Rafe's uncomplicated request. She cracked one eye open, hoping to get a hint of how angry he was before she fully committed to dropping the whole if-I-can't-see-you-you-can't-see-me farce.

Not a trace of anger lingered in Rafe's gray-green eyes. He was perched on the very edge of the sofa, leaning toward her with his elbows on his knees. As if he wasn't sure whether he should spring into action or give her some space.

Relief washed over her skin, like jumping into a pool on a humid, sweaty day. "I'm sorry," she whispered, opening her eyes the rest of the way.

He was on his feet and at her side in the blink of an eye. "Did I say something wrong?"

Something about him made her take a step back, studying him. It took her several seconds to figure out what she found so astonishing. She realized he felt honest-to-God, genuine guilt.

The pain in his voice and eyes. The way he kept raising a hand to touch her before forcing it back to his side. His posture, which was, for the first time since she met him, less than perfect.

He hurt her in a way he didn't intend, and he actually gave a fuck. Brian would've shrugged it off or scolded her for overreacting. As for Micah, he would have said all the right words in the beginning, but the regret in his eyes would've been entirely fake. She learned to tell the difference after a while . . . and he hadn't bothered pretending after that.

"You didn't say anything wrong," she told him, wanting to make the deep lines in his forehead disappear. "At least, not on purpose. There's no way you could've known."

When he stepped closer to her that time, lifting a hand tentatively toward her face, she didn't back away. His hand was so big and warm and strong against her cheek, and it felt so fucking good. She had to resist the urge to rub up against him like a cat.

"Do you think you can explain it?" Something between them shifted last night. She'd never heard such softness in his voice. "Or would you rather not talk about it?"

"No, I"—she gulped, trying to swallow down a lump of fear in her throat—"really want to explain. I'm so sorry for freaking out like that."

Rafe brushed his thumb back and forth along her cheekbone. "Remember the deal we made about apologizing?"

To be completely honest, she'd forgotten entirely. "Right. I'm not supposed to say I'm sorry unless you tell me to."

"And have I told you to?" he asked, one corner of his mouth lifting into a teasing smile.

Her smile was equal parts sheepish and pleased. "No, Sir, you haven't."

"All right then." He moved his thumb lower, sweeping it along her bottom lip. "Carry on."

"Micah used to say something a lot like what you said." She flinched at the sudden hardening of his eyes, but forced herself to keep going. "He always said, 'Just do as I say. It's not that fucking complicated.' And the tone was similar, though I swear I know you weren't actually saying it like him at all. You're nothing like him. It just sounded the same, and I—"

He silenced her with the softest, gentlest of kisses. "Dismissing you without even listening was wrong of me, whether it makes me anything like Micah or not. I won't do it again."

There was a dewy, lovesick look on her face. She knew it beyond a shadow of a doubt. And there was nothing in the world she could do about it. Rafe Erikson was unlike any other man she'd ever met, and she better start being extra fucking careful before she went and caught even more feelings.

"Now." He pulled away at last, giving her a little space so she could compose herself. "Why don't you tell me what's wrong so we can figure out how to fix it."

"I was trying to get ready without waking you this morning, so I didn't want to go digging around in my bag." At his uncomprehending look, she added, "I'm not wearing anything under this."

His lips spread into a slow, wicked smile. "Is that so." Reaching up, he brushed his thumb across her nipple, making it harden beneath the thin cotton. It only made him smile wider. "That's not a problem at all. In fact, it's the best news I've heard all morning."

Nell rolled her eyes toward the ceiling. "Ha ha."

But it was abundantly clear he wasn't joking. Fondling her other breast outright, his voice was a little rougher than normal when he said, "Permission to go upstairs denied. I want you naked today."

Butterflies took flight in her stomach, and she was straight-up squirming with desire. She might not be able to do her whole meditation/emptying her mind thing this time. Not if every inch of her would be on lewd display. It was as if he twisted the dial of her lust all the way up to the highest setting. And yet he stepped away, no longer touching or teasing, leaving her aching for more.

Why did she have a feeling that was exactly what he wanted?

Stripping off her clothes, she folded them carefully and placed them on the seat of an armchair that matched the sofa. No sooner had she gotten into position on the floor, Rafe reclining on the sofa with his feet resting on the center of her back, than footsteps sounded behind her.

Nell's face burned with shame, knowing all her most intimate places were one hundred percent visible to this unknown person. If it was Mason . . . well, that would be okay. He'd seen every inch of her already. But it could be anyone walking through that door.

The rest of her body summarily ignored her prudish brain, and she found herself spreading her legs a tiny bit wider, hoping to improve the view.

Jesus, she was such a perv.

When the mystery person walked into her line of sight, it was a man in his late twenties or so, wearing a white chef's jacket. The silver tray in his hands held what she assumed to be a mug of Rafe's usual black coffee and a tall, narrow glass with an iced chai tea latte, like the one she chose the previous morning.

Their gazes met for only a moment, and he smirked. The man focused on Rafe as he set the tray down on a side table. "As requested, your coffee and tea."

"Thank you, Luca." Rafe sounded distracted—not surprising, since he was tapping away at his laptop already.

Luca gave her one more salacious look before he hurried from the room.

Fucking hell, she was about ready to abandon her task and reach back to touch herself, and all she did was make eye contact with a member of the kitchen staff. What would happen if one of the other Doms walked in?

Especially if it was Mason. After yesterday, she might spontaneously combust.

Whether he knew how much she suffered, or he was simply in a hurry, she didn't know. But Rafe didn't linger over his coffee that morning, emptying the mug in a matter of minutes. Lowering his feet to the floor, he motioned for her to kneel up like usual. Nell's gaze automatically moved to the laptop, expecting him to spin it around like previous mornings.

Instead, he handed her a small rectangle of paper. "I meant to give this to you yesterday, but I was distracted."

She looked down at it for several long seconds, uncomprehending. It was the check Mason wrote on Tuesday—the one she saw him hand to Rafe after the auction. She'd assumed it was a prop, all part of the performance.

But this check looked remarkably real. And it was made out to her.

Nell looked up at Rafe, her mouth working but no words coming out. Finally, she managed a strained, "I don't understand."

"We usually donate the money from these kinds of things to charity." He said it like he was telling her why he preferred coffee over tea—not at all like he was explaining why there was a legit check for fifteen grand in her hand.

These things? As in, they auctioned off girls at the Manor before? *For actual fucking money?*

Damn, maybe the eye hooks had been on the ceiling the whole time after all.

Not seeming to notice the way her thoughts spun around and around like they were caught in a whirlpool, Rafe kept right on talking. "But given how hard you've been working to rebuild your life, and because you're probably going back to school soon, we all agreed to make an exception this time." With a smirk, he added, "Besides, Mason and Gemma said you more than earned it."

Nell continued staring down at the check, her eyes stinging with the threat of tears. No way this was really happening. It was too good to be true.

Rafe finally seemed to notice something was off. "Are you okay?" He sounded confused more than concerned.

"Is this real?" There was such raw hope in her voice, it was embarrassing. For the first time since her arrival, she felt like she didn't belong here. Like this beautiful place and the beautiful people who filled it were entirely out of her league.

"Of course it's real." Rafe frowned down at her, a deep line between his brows. "Why wouldn't it be?"

She took a moment to think of the most diplomatic way to answer. After a long, uncomfortable pause, she settled on, "You do realize this is almost ten times what I paid to come here, right?"

"Ah." For the first time since she met him, he actually looked embarrassed. Running a hand through his hair, he reached for his coffee mug, only to let it drop awkwardly back onto the table when he remembered it was empty.

Watching him fidget with shrewd eyes, Nell asked, "Did Mistress Freya talk you into giving me a major discount? Or did she pay most of my way?"

With a smile that very clearly said, *Oops, you caught me*, he said, "A little of both. Freya didn't think you'd come if you knew she paid for it, but she wouldn't let me work for such a reduced rate either. So we compromised. Trust me, it's not a big deal."

Yeah, no, she wasn't letting him off that easy. It may not be a big deal to him or Freya, but it was sure as fuck a big deal to her. "How much do people usually pay?"

He tilted his head toward the check in her still-outstretched hand. "Enough for that amount of money not to phase most of the people here."

Staring back down at the life-altering check, Nell muttered, "Jesus Christ."

"Nell, it's okay," he said, hauling her up onto his lap, holding her tight against his chest. "Use it to pay for your school."

"But I can't really take Mason's money, can I?" Fuck, she wanted to. But it felt so wrong. "I mean, he did *me* a favor, fulfilling my fantasy. And now he has to give me fifteen grand on top of it? Why would he agree to that?"

Rafe made a sound that was half consoling, half apologetic. "I didn't tell the others how much to bid on you. They knew it was real, and they decided that's what they were willing to pay for you to be their slave for an hour."

"Really?" She couldn't help the disbelief in her voice. Why would anyone pay so much for an hour with her? It was fucking absurd.

"I'm serious," Rafe insisted. "So you have nothing to feel guilty or weird about, okay? Take that money and use it to help pay for your master's degree. When I told them you were thinking of becoming a therapist to help abused women, they were impressed as fuck. No wonder they bid so high. The more people like you we have out there, the better the world will be."

Tears were building in her eyes. "Thank you. This is too good to be true."

Kissing the soft spot behind her ear, Rafe pulled the laptop across her thighs. "Now get to work. Time for you to figure out how to change the world." He lowered his voice to a whisper when he added, "And don't forget, I owe you a spanking."

Nell's lips curled into an excited smile. As if she possibly could.

CHAPTER 14
Rafe

W ell, fuck.

After she worked on some grad school applications, Rafe gave Nell his phone and sent her out into the garden to call her sister. Last time he checked, she'd been wandering around the stone pathways with a radiant smile on her face.

Now she was huddled on one of the benches, his phone on the seat beside her.

Rafe was through the French back doors and across the flagstone patio in a matter of seconds. She didn't look up as he approached.

Placing a tentative hand on her shoulder, he waited until she leaned into him to slide his hand up into her hair. He ran gentle, soothing fingers along her scalp several times before asking, "What happened?"

"Holly and Pete had dinner with my parents last night." She closed her eyes, sending a pair of tears down her cheeks. "As far as they're concerned, I died ten years ago."

Ah. So it went about as well as everyone expected. "She said it would probably take some time."

With a slow, forlorn nod, Nell said, "Yeah, I know. I couldn't really help getting my hopes up anyway."

Settling on the bench, he pulled Nell into his lap, holding her tight against his chest. "Parents are supposed to love their children unconditionally." He spoke the words softly into her hair. "I barely know your sister, but I know her well enough to be sure she'll remind them of that every chance she gets until they wise up."

She couldn't manage more than a weak laugh. "That's true."

As he racked his brain for a way to console her, a butterfly fluttered over to a patch of asters, landing on one of the purple flowers. Its large black wings had rows of white and yellow-orange spots, with little smudges of a soft, iridescent blue.

"Look," he said, pointing at the beautiful, delicate creature. "Remember what you told me? About wrapping yourself up in all your choices like a cocoon?"

She watched the butterfly gather its nectar, a soft, faraway look in her eyes. "I remember."

"Then the whole thing falls away, and there you are, completely transformed."

"New Dom, new safeword, new me," she whispered.

"Yes!" His enthusiasm startled her, and he kissed the soft spot behind her ear before continuing in a calmer voice. "That's exactly my point. How do you know you're not transforming already?"

Nell half-turned her head, as if to make sure she'd be able to hear his next words.

"You're not the same person you were ten years ago. The Nell I know would never let Micah treat you the way he did. You'd break his fucking nose."

Her mouth twitched.

"You're not even the Nell who came here five days ago. That woman was afraid of her scars. Ashamed of them." He lifted the hem of her black, asymmetrical top, spreading his fingers across her taut belly. "Look how much color you got tanning with Olivia yesterday. *My* Nell knows there's absolutely nothing to be fucking ashamed of."

Nell turned back toward the butterfly, frowning as she considered his words. It wasn't until the insect drifted away in search of new flowers that she balled her hands into tight fists. "If the parents of serial killers can still love them, my parents can definitely still love me. Especially since basically all I did was have sex in a way that embarrassed them."

God, he loved the fire in her voice. "Abso-fucking-lutely. They think your relationship was shameful, but for all the wrong fucking reasons. The only person who needs to be ashamed of what they did is Micah. Don't you ever forget that."

When she twisted around to look at him, the adoration in her eyes stole his breath. Not a soul in the world had ever looked at him like that. Not even Jess.

Needing to taste her, Rafe crushed his lips against hers, holding onto her so tightly she whimpered into his mouth. He devoured the tiny sound, wanting every single bit of her he could possibly get. Fucking hell, he'd never be able to get enough.

Shoving the fact that she would leave Fairford Manor in two days to the back of his mind, he lost himself in the moment. She tasted spicy and sweet at the same time, like cinnamon and cloves. With her sun ripened peach smell, the silky feel of her in his hands, and her little gasps and moans . . . Jesus fucking Christ, she overwhelmed his senses.

"Come on," he said before he lost himself completely, standing and placing her on her feet.

She followed without question, into the house and to the end of the hallway, where he punched a six-digit code into the keypad by the dungeon door. Relief flooded through him when they made it to the bottom of the stairs, finding the dungeon empty. He didn't want any interruptions or distractions.

Rafe led her straight to the Shibari corner of the dungeon, which housed the enormous wooden suspension rig Aiden helped him build a few years ago. It almost looked like monkey bars from a child's playground, with thick wooden slats running across the top and down both sides. Heavy duty forged anchor rings were strategically mounted all over the rig, the metal shining against the black-stained wood.

Leaving Nell standing beneath the rig's upper bars, he headed to the nearby wall, where dozens of lengths of rope hung from hooks. The nylon and cotton braided ropes came in endless colors, all stored in identical, perfect bundles. Rafe led a mandatory class with the other Doms on the proper cleaning and storing of his rope as soon as they installed the suspension rig.

Ignoring the flashier options, he chose the two longest lengths of the stronger, undyed hemp bondage rope. He only hoped they were long enough for what he had in mind.

He carried his supplies back to Nell, arranging the bundles side-by-side at her feet. She didn't speak as he stripped off her jeans and shirt, tossing the clothes aside.

"Beautiful," he said, admiring the black strapless bra and matching panties underneath. "Stand with your legs together and your arms at your sides."

She did as she was told, flattening her arms and hands against her sides when he pressed against them. "Like this, Sir?"

Rafe ran the tips of his fingers along her cheekbone. "That's perfect. Now try not to move." Unwrapping the two bundles of hemp rope, he got to work.

There were few things he found quite as calming as Shibari. The repetition as he created each perfect knot, the precision and patience required to turn his sub into a work of art with only the rope in his hands and his imagination to guide him . . . it mesmerized him.

He created dozens of crossing hitches, using the simple knot to connect the two ropes in a patchwork pattern across her skin, enveloping her body from her shoulders down. By the time he finished with a double column tie at her ankles, she was encased in a cocoon of rope, completely immobilized.

"So fucking beautiful," he murmured as he circled her. With a single fingertip, he traced her skin just inside the square of rope between her shoulder blades, a knot at each of the four corners. He did the same inside a square over her hip, and then the center of her chest, directly above her breasts. "Do you understand what I'm doing?"

Her smile made his heart skip a beat. "You're turning me into a butterfly."

Rafe brushed a gentle kiss over her lips. "Good girl. Are you ready for the cocoon to unravel?"

She closed her eyes, taking as deep a breath as her binds would allow. "Yes, Sir."

Standing straight and tall, she didn't move a muscle as he undid his work one knot at a time. When at last he was done, he helped her step over the discarded rope to the new life waiting beyond.

When Rafe found out Nell and Zach secretly planned a Halloween party, he didn't know whether to laugh or turn her over his knee.

He settled on both.

But when he and Nell walked into the parlor, it was impossible to not be impressed. The space had been so utterly transformed, it looked like something out of a Tim Burton movie.

Black spiderwebs covered the white walls, only hints of the picture frame molding and intricately carved chair rail peeking through. The blue velvet furniture was draped in a shimmering gray fabric, festooned in sprays of black and orange silk flowers woven through twisting black vines. Black metal lanterns that used to be on the front porch hung from hooks in the ceiling, and a spectacular assortment of jack-o-lanterns were clustered on tables and along the walls, candles flickering out of each terrifying face.

And it looked like not a single invitation had been declined. Holy fuck, even Leo and Sophie drove up from Manhattan. How Nell and Zach pulled all this together in only a day was quite beyond him.

Rafe's jaw still hung open when Jonathan sauntered up to them in a pirate costume, the scantily clad brunette on his arm dressed as a bar wench. "So. The ringleader has arrived at last."

"Nell, this is Jonathan. The Manor's senior founding partner." He couldn't help smirking when she squirmed.

Nell blushed under the other Dom's scrutiny, not quite able to meet his gaze. "Zach told you the party was my idea?" Despite the trepidation in her voice, she was trying to hide a smile.

"He did indeed." Jonathan moved his shrewd gaze over to Rafe. "I hope you punished her soundly for all this nonsense."

Rafe only grinned in response. It was good to see someone keeping Jonathan on his toes. If anyone in this place relaxed less than he did, it was Jonathan. Even Mason took time off every couple of months to travel.

The man desperately needed a night of fun.

Jonathan's sub couldn't have been more different. She beamed as she looked around the room, taking in the decorations and costumes, practically bouncing on her toes in excitement. "I'm going to go get another drink, Sir," she said, wending off toward the refreshment table.

Rafe followed her progress through the room with his eyes, then glanced around at the other subs. They all wore similar expressions. Perhaps Nell and Zach were onto something with this whole party idea.

"Speak of the devil," Nell said as Zach sidled up to their group dressed as Geralt, complete with replica longsword and a shoulder-length white wig. The armor made even his lean shoulders look huge. "I like all the black leather. Very appropriate."

He smirked at her. "I told you I was coming dressed as my one true love." Giving her black leather corset, matching mini-skirt, and opaque black stockings a once-over, he said, "I thought you were coming as Sexy Red Riding Hood, so Rafe could be your wolf."

"That idea was vetoed." Nell rolled her eyes in Rafe's direction. "In fact, I was informed I would be attending the party as a cat or not at all."

Rafe smiled and straightened her fluffy black cat ears. "I needed my familiar," he said, though it was a bald-faced lie. He came up with the wizard costume idea at least an hour after deciding she needed to be his little kitten for the night.

"Is the tail attached to the skirt, or . . ." Zach let the question trail off.

With an exaggerated wink, Nell said, "Wouldn't you like to know."

God, it felt good to laugh. And not only that, but to laugh with a whole group of others. It had been years since he let down his guard this much—since before Jess died.

"I better go find out where my naughty little sub has run off to," Jonathan said, still smiling. "Enjoy yourselves tonight."

Only seconds later, Zach leaned in to give Nell a hug, whispering something in her ear. She smacked his arm as he retreated, hurrying over to where Gabriel was telling a story in the ridiculous French accent he insisted on using in front of guests. Apparently he thought it made him seem like a more legit chef or something equally absurd.

Rafe leaned down to whisper in Nell's ear. "What'd he say?"

Her cheeks turned a brilliant scarlet under her painted whiskers.

"He said to be a good little kitty so I could have some cream at the end of the night."

Roaring with laughter, Rafe swung her around for a kiss. "Thank you for this," he said as they broke apart. "I haven't had this much fun in . . . well, forever, honestly."

Nell's answering grin was mischievous. "Just wait until the party games start."

"Normal party games?" he asked, arching an eyebrow. "Or kinky party games?"

She scoffed. "Of course they're kinky. This is Fairford Manor. You guys have a reputation to uphold."

"Good lord." He shook his head but grinned from ear to ear. "I'm not even sure I want to know. Now be a good girl and say hello to Leo and Sophie."

The Manor's silent partner and his wife had been making their rounds, and both smiled as they approached. "Rafe, good to see you again," Leo said, holding out a hand.

Rafe shook the other man's hand, then leaned in to plant a chaste kiss on Sophie's cheek. "This is Leo," he told Nell, gesturing to the sandy haired, blue eyed golden boy. Seriously, the man looked like he belonged on a fifty-foot sailboat, or maybe the cover of a magazine about horses. "He founded the Manor with Jonathan, Mason, and Aiden, but as a silent partner. And this is his wife, Sophie." Wrapping a possessive arm around his sub's shoulders, he beamed at them. "And this is Nell."

"Oh, we know." Leaning in to give Nell a hug, Sophie said in a stage whisper, "We've heard all about you from Jonathan and Mason. They won't stop complaining about you planning this party, but I can tell they secretly love it."

When Sophie pulled away, the look on Nell's face was equal parts stunned and pleased. "Oh, I, umm . . ." She was so fucking adorable when she was flustered. "I *love* your costume," she finally got out, and he could practically see hearts in her eyes as she looked at Sophie.

Hmm. First Gemma, now Sophie. Apparently she had a thing for gorgeous blondes. Good to know.

Sophie grinned back, smoothing down the front of her already pristine Wonder Woman outfit. It wasn't a cheap polyester costume from one of those pop-up Halloween stores. No, this thing looked like it came straight out of the movie and fit like it had been made for her.

Considering how loaded he suspected the pair of them were, it probably had been. Not as much went into Leo's Superman costume, of course, but it too was clearly custom made. Rafe suspected he looked like an idiot in a bathrobe and a silly pointy hat by comparison.

The most beautiful woman in the room was there with him, though. So he honestly didn't give a flying fuck.

As the two women obsessed over everyone's outfits like they were best friends, not perfect strangers, Rafe did his best at having a polite conversation with Leo. Small talk wasn't exactly his strong suit—he fucking hated it, in fact—but he found himself wishing he knew these people better than he did. He had to start somewhere, right?

The pair didn't come up to Fairford often, especially after the birth of their daughter two years ago. Even when one or both made the drive, it was always for a meeting or some other less frivolous occasion. He never got a chance to just sit and chat like this, and actually get to know them as people rather than business partners.

The original founders had all been friends in college, and came up with the whole idea for the Manor shortly before they graduated. Apparently Sophie was the real estate agent who sold them the property some years later. Rafe didn't know if it was love at first sight or what; he never got the full story. All he knew was that Leo switched from partner to silent partner before the Manor even opened for business, never taking a single client.

The easy way the four founding partners always conversed when they got together left Rafe feeling like an outsider at every single meeting. It was long past time for that to change.

Though he didn't see how the current conversation would help much. It started off well, with Rafe asking about their daughter's latest birthday party and life in the city. But in the last minute or so, it somehow morphed into a deep dive into the current state of the stock market—something Rafe knew next to nothing about. Then Nell slipped out to use the bathroom, the traitor, leaving him to wade through this mess alone.

Christ, this was awkward. Especially when Leo gave him a puzzled look after his latest attempt to take an active part in the conversation.

Fuck it.

With a lopsided grin, he said, "I guess you can tell I have absolutely no idea what I'm talking about."

Leo cracked a smile, and Sophie laughed. "I had my suspicions," he said, having the good grace to look chagrined. "Sorry, I didn't mean to bore you to death."

Sophie leaned her head against her husband's shoulder. "He does this all the time. You just have to be willing to tell him to shut up."

"Watch it," Leo said, giving her bottom a single hard smack. "Unless you want me to punish you in front of all these people."

She didn't seem remotely phased by the threat. "Rafe, I've got to say, you're much more relaxed than I've ever seen you." Her brown eyes sparkled with intrigue. "Perhaps the doing of a certain tall brunette?"

Rafe's cheeks heated, and it took him a second to realize why.

He was actually fucking blushing. Since when did Rafe Erikson *blush*?

"Well, well," Leo drawled, grinning. "Isn't that an interesting development."

Oh, for fuck's sake. He had no idea what would happen with Nell, and he was pretty damn sure continued public humiliation wouldn't help him figure it out.

Their connection was intense, sure. Infinitely more than he ever felt with another woman, Jess included. But if all went according to the current plan, she would head back to Tampa tomorrow morning, and that would be that.

So ask her to stay.

The thought had been lurking around in the back of his mind since last night. But since it was certifiably fucking insane, he ignored it completely—something that was harder to do with Sophie and Leo grinning at him like they were already planning his wedding.

Time for a hasty and awkward retreat.

"I need to head to the bathroom, too," Rafe said, half turning toward the doorway. "I'll catch up with you guys in a little bit."

The pair gave each other a knowing look that spoke volumes. He fucking hated it.

Trying to pretend this wasn't the most confusing and mortifying conversation of his life, Rafe headed out into the hall with unhurried steps. He didn't want it to look like he was running away, even though the other two clearly knew the truth.

He waited until the parlor was out of sight before leaning against a wall and closing his eyes. What in the actual fuck was he going to do?

Okay, it was time to be completely honest with himself once and for all. He didn't want Nell to leave.

There. He finally fucking admitted it.

He couldn't hear wedding bells like Leo and Sophie, but his feelings were real. They were the most intensely real and important thing in his life.

Which meant letting her check out tomorrow and walk out of his life as if this was just another week was out of the question. He at least had to find out if she felt the same way first. If so, they could figure out next steps together. If not . . . well, he'd cross that bridge when he came to it.

Mind made up, he hurried down the hall to the bathroom with long strides. There was no point in waiting. If she was going to rip his heart out of his chest, he'd rather get it over with.

Rafe knocked on the bathroom door as soon as he reached it. "Nell, are you almost done? I need to talk to you about something."

There was no answer.

He frowned at the light coming through the crack under the door. It looked like she was still in there, but it had been several minutes since she excused herself from the party. "Nell?" He knocked louder that time, just in case.

When the bathroom remained silent, he tried the handle. Unlocked. And there wasn't a soul inside.

His frown deepened. Nell hadn't returned to the party—he was absolutely sure of that. He'd been standing right by the doorway, and he would've passed her in the hall on his way here.

Maybe she ran up to their suite to grab something?

With no other ideas, he made his way down the rest of the hallway and out to the lobby. He'd just rounded the corner and climbed the first stair when something caught his attention out of the corner of his eye. Turning, he looked across the cavernous room, past the reception desk to the closed door beyond.

Light shone out of the crack under that door, too, but he knew Zach wasn't in there. He saw him as he left the party, laughing with Olivia, Gabriel, and Gabriel's sous chef Sienna.

It was probably nothing. Zach must've left the light on by mistake.

But he couldn't shake the feeling that something was off. Particularly since he couldn't remember the last time he saw that door closed.

The rubber soles of his boots didn't make a sound as he crossed the marble tiles. Slipping around the edge of the reception desk, he opened the door without knocking.

Nell jumped so hard, the desk chair rolled backward into the mail table, making the shelves wobble ominously. "Jesus!" She slapped a hand over her heart. "You scared the shit out of me."

Resisting the urge to comfort her, he kept his voice neutral as he said, "I thought you were going to the bathroom."

"I was." A hint of color appeared along her cheekbones. "I mean, I did. I was just taking a minute before I went back in there. It was kind of overwhelming."

Rafe's gaze flicked toward the open laptop on Zach's desk. The screen faced away from him. "Were you using Zach's computer?"

"No." The blush covered her entire face now.

"And what if I asked you about stealing my phone Monday night?" Why she thought she could get away with such a ridiculous lie was quite beyond him. She must have been itching for a spanking. "What would your answer be to that?"

Her mouth opened and closed a few times, but no sound came out.

"I'm going to ask you again. And this time I want you to tell me the truth." His mind raced with possibilities. Punish her right here, or march her back into the party and put on a bit of a show? He supposed that depended on the reason she was sneaking around. "Were you using Zach's computer?"

Lower lip trembling, she whispered, "Yes, Sir."

"Why?"

"I wanted to check my email. But I haven't even signed in yet. I'll turn the computer off and—"

"Stop."

She'd started inching toward the desk, but froze at his harsh tone, one hand still outstretched. Only her eyes moved, shifting back and forth between him and the laptop.

Nell shrank back in the chair as he went to the desk, spinning the laptop to face him. As he expected, she was already signed into her email. But it wasn't the same one he'd seen her using all week. The background was plain black; the other inbox had a picture of a beach.

Forehead creasing, he leaned down for a closer look. When he saw the email at the top of the inbox, the blood in his veins ran cold as ice.

The sender was Micah O'Neill. For one fleeting second, he held onto hope. Who gave a shit if Micah emailed her. That didn't mean anything. But then he read the preview: *It's time for us to stop emailing and meet face to face. I don'*...

His gaze raked down her inbox, finding her ex's name two other times. Both emails were marked as read.

His gaze bore into hers with such intensity she flinched. "You've been emailing Micah."

"No!" She surged to her feet as she said it, reaching for him with both hands.

Grabbing her wrists, he held her several inches away. "Don't fucking lie to me."

"He's been emailing me ever since I left. But I never emailed him back, I swear. The rest of his emails are in the trash. You can see for yourself." Desperation added an edge to her voice. A plea burned in her eyes. And he had absolutely no idea if any of it was real.

"Okay. I'll see for myself." He flung her away from him with enough force that she toppled into the chair. It rolled backward against the table again, making envelopes flutter down to the floor. But he didn't open her trash folder. Instead, Rafe clicked on the oldest read email—the first of three with the subject line *I see you found all my emails at last.* "Dearest Noelle," he read aloud in a mocking voice. "I can't tell you what a relief it is to know you're safe. I've worried each and every moment since the day you disappeared."

158

"Rafe, I didn't—"

"Oh, look, he's been going to *therapy*," he interrupted, his gaze skipping down near the end. "How touching. Obviously he loves you enough to stop being a psychopath, just for you."

She was crying when she next spoke. "I know I shouldn't have read the emails. But I fucking swear, I don't want anything to do with him."

"Clearly," Rafe ground out, facing her again. "That's why you hacked into my phone and Zach's computer to read his emails. Because he means nothing at all to you anymore." He must be the biggest fucking idiot in the world, coming in here to confess he was—what? In love with her?

Absolutely fucking not. He learned his lesson eighteen years ago. If he let himself feel, if he gave up even a hint of control, he got hurt.

Jesus, he needed to get the fuck out of here. Whirling around, he practically ran from the tiny office.

"Rafe! *Please!*" Her shouts chased him from the room, only making his legs move faster. "Let me explain."

But he was done listening. He went right through the front doors with only one thought on his mind. He needed to get the fuck away from Fairford Manor as quickly as he could.

CHAPTER 15
Nell

Her heart was fucking breaking. She could literally feel it in her chest, cracks surging through it as if it were made of porcelain instead of tissue and blood.

Nell survived a decade in hell to get here. For one beautiful, shimmering moment, it had all seemed worth it. Every cruel word, every scar. She'd do it all over again if it meant ending up here . . . with Rafe.

And now she lost him, because she was too fucking stupid to leave the past where it belonged. The new life she imagined while Rafe wrapped her in his rope cocoon ended before it ever really started.

She had no idea how long she cried in that chair. It could've been minutes or hours. All she knew was that she needed Rafe to change his mind. To come back. Listen. Believe. And then give her another chance. She needed it more than she needed her next gasping breath.

But she knew he wouldn't come.

When at last her tears dried out, she tried to force herself to think. To plan her next steps. She needed to lose herself in logic right now, before her emotions could swallow her whole.

There was no way she could stay here. Not with a party full of people who were surely already wondering where she and Rafe disappeared to. She couldn't face them—their inevitable questions, and their condemnation when they learned how she hurt their friend.

Her flight to Florida didn't leave until tomorrow afternoon. Would an airport as small as the one in New Hampshire stay open all night? If not, there had to be a twenty-four-hour diner nearby, right?

Dale's card was still stuffed into the side pocket of her purse, and he promised to come get her anytime, day or night. All she had to do was avoid the others for the next three hours so he had time to drive up to Fairford.

Three stupid, tortuous hours. She cursed this state and its lack of a decent airport. The one in Burlington was so tiny, it would've cost three times as much to fly there, and involved a huge layover instead of a direct flight.

As far as plans went, this one wasn't great. It didn't fix anything at all. But at least it protected her from even more pain. That would have to do for now.

Trying to ignore the way her insides twisted and writhed, she scooted the chair up to Zach's desk. As soon as she logged out of his computer, she'd go upstairs to pack.

She sort of told the truth before. When Rafe burst into the room, she'd only just logged in. She hadn't gotten a chance to look as her inbox loaded. At the very top was the email from Micah he undoubtably saw, which had arrived less than an hour ago. No way was she reading that, ever. She would sign out of this account and never check it again for as long as she fucking lived.

But before she could follow through on the thought, another name caught her eye. Leslie Beaumont.

Her mother.

She got an email from *her mom*.

Nell didn't know if she was holding her breath, or if she forgot how to breathe. She leaned closer to the screen as she clicked on it.

Dear Noelle,

I don't really know how to start this email. It doesn't feel real somehow, talking to you again after so many years. I've been sitting here for over an hour staring at the screen, trying to figure it out.

The most important thing I need to say is that you're my daughter no matter what, and I'll always love you. I don't think I'll ever understand the decisions you've made, but maybe I don't have to. As long as you're safe and happy now, that'll have to be enough for me.

I'm sorry I didn't come with Holly and the others when they tried to help you. All these years I've wondered if it would've gone differently if I was there. If I could've said something that made a difference and saved you so much pain. I failed you before. But I'm not going to fail you again.

I'm so, so proud of you for leaving that monster on your own.

Holly told me all about this Fairford Manor place you're at, and explained all the ways this is different. She said she likes this Rafe person you're with now. I still don't entirely understand, but I'm trying to. And I'll keep trying until I do. That's my promise to you.

Your dad is going to take longer to convince. I told him tonight that he should be on his knees every day for the rest of his life, thanking God for bringing you back to us. Holly and I will convince him in the end. Hang in there.

Please call me when you can. I need to hear your voice. I need to see you and hold you. I need to know beyond a shadow of a doubt that my baby girl is okay.

Love,

Mom

Nell was crying again by the time she finished reading. Not only from the joy and relief of having her mom back, though that was a huge part of it. But from realizing she'd never get to introduce Rafe to her family. They'd never know the man who helped her find her way back to them. That loss made the whole thing hurt even worse.

She was about to log out when she froze, her eyes going wide, her heart pounding. *Holly told me all about this Fairford Manor place you're at.*

Micah had been checking her emails. If he read the email—if he knew where she was . . .

"Shit!"

The email from her mom had arrived at 10:02 the previous night. Almost twenty-four hours for him to read the message. Almost twenty-four hours to act.

Her hand shook so hard as she tried to open Micah's latest email, she missed on her first three attempts. She screamed, "Goddamnit!" at the computer, as if that would somehow help. Why the fuck hadn't she changed her password? It hadn't seemed to matter at the time; she never expected to get emails from anyone but him. But now it felt like one more stupid mistake—the cherry on top of her idiot sundae.

When at last she got the fucking thing open, her heart stopped beating in her chest. Beneath several paragraphs of text, part of a picture was visible. She scrolled down until the image filled the screen.

It had been nearly a decade since she last saw Holly, but the woman in the photo was unmistakably her sister, her hair shoulder length now instead of long, the beginnings of crow's feet around her eyes. Holly was in front of a large gambrel-style house, blue with black shutters, with a small boy who was presumably Nell's nephew Justin. They both laughed as they played in a pile of fall leaves.

The photo had been taken from inside a car, with a slight glare from the window. A face was reflected in the side mirror.

She recognized the square jaw, stubby nose, and dark, wide-set eyes. He was a friend of Micah's from L.A. Doug had always been willing when Micah wanted an audience while he hurt her.

"No, no, no, no, no . . ." She kept whispering it as she scrolled to the top, terrified of what she'd find.

Noelle,

It's time for us to stop emailing and meet face to face. I don't know why you ever thought you could get away from me for good. You're mine. You'll always be fucking mine. How dare you let another man touch my property, you dirty little whore. By the time I'm through with you, no other man will ever want to touch you again.

I've come to Vermont to collect you. If you come to me like a good girl, no one but you needs to be punished. But if you don't, as you can see, I know where your sister lives. Doug is parked down the street right now, waiting to hear from me. If you don't do as I tell you, your sister and nephew will receive the punishment that should've been yours.

Come to the trail behind the pool at this ridiculous fucking mansion. Come alone. If I suspect there's even a chance you told anyone or called the police, Holly and the kid will be gone long before the cops can get to them. You have until 9PM to make your decision.

I'm waiting.

Master

As soon as she finished reading, her gaze flicked down to the bottom right corner of the screen. It was 8:53. And Holly's number was stored on Rafe's phone, nowhere else.

Nell sprinted from the room as fast as her legs would carry her.

The buzzing of insects made the woods seem deceptively peaceful. But she wasn't fooled. She knew there was a monster lurking in the dark.

It must have been a new moon, for the only traces of light came from the blue glow of the pool. Her steps slowed as the darkness surrounded her, but she didn't let herself stop. There wasn't any time.

Nell only made it about ten feet down the wide hiking trail before Micah appeared, stepping out from behind the thick trunk of a tree.

"I was starting to think you weren't coming." A hint of a smirk was visible in the faint light from the pool. "But I should've known. You were always so predictable."

Hearing his voice again was like being doused with a bucket of ice water. Every instinct in her body told her to run. Get the fuck out of there and never look back.

She took a single, tiny step closer. "Tell Doug I'm here." She cleared her throat, wanting to sound stronger, braver, but it didn't do any good. "Tell him to leave Holly and Justin alone."

Micah threw back his head and laughed. God, it was a chilling sound. She loved this man once. Obsessed over him. Gave herself to him in every way possible. The very idea made bile rise in her throat.

"I'm not joking, Micah." There couldn't be more than thirty seconds left before nine. "I did what you said. Call your fucking friend off."

The humor drained out of him as she spoke. "You fucking whore. How dare you speak to your Master that way."

"I'm not—"

But he didn't give her a chance to finish her objection. "Enough! Unless you want your sister's blood on your hands, I suggest you get on your knees and fucking *beg* me to forgive you."

Absolutely fucking not.

The words were right there on the tip of her tongue, but she couldn't make herself say them. Not until he made that goddamn phone call.

Swallowing down the vomit clawing its way up her throat, she dropped slowly to her knees. "Please forgive me, Master." She almost gagged on the words and had to force herself to keep going. "I know I shouldn't speak to you that way. It was my fear for Holly and Justin talking. I'll never forget my place again."

He took slow, prowling steps toward her, a look of utmost satisfaction on his face. "And what is your place, Noelle?"

Nell longed to close her eyes. To shut all this out, pretend it wasn't happening, disappear.

Not. An. Option.

"Whatever you want it to be, Master."

He hummed his approval. "Good. Perhaps you haven't been away too long after all. I won't need to completely retrain you."

When Micah circled around behind her, she had to dig her fingernails into her cuticles, focusing on the sharp pain to keep herself from turning around. Doing it would only make him lash out; she'd learned that years ago. She had to keep him calm for as long as humanly possible.

She couldn't help jerking away when he slipped his hand beneath her hair, brushing his fingers against her neck. It made every inch of her skin crawl, as if a colony of ants had taken up residence inside her.

Micah grabbed a fistful of her hair, yanking her head back. "Don't you dare pull away from me, you little cunt. You're mine. Mine to touch, mine to punish, mine to fuck. You're only alive because I *want* you to be alive. Don't you ever fucking forget it, or I can change my mind like that." He snapped his fingers right in front of her eyes, making her flinch.

"I'm sorry, Master," she whispered, blinking back tears. "I didn't mean to. I was startled. That's all. I'm so sorry."

Fucking fuck, she had to keep him *calm*. Her body needed to stop betraying her if she wanted any chance of everyone surviving this unscathed.

She locked all her muscles, willing them to remain immobile no matter what. "I'm yours to command, Master. Please instruct me on how best to serve you."

His thin lips lifted into the shape of a smile. "So you haven't forgotten."

"Never, Master." Her tears were hot against her skin. "I'll never forget."

Reaching out with his free hand, he traced a fingernail along her jawline. It felt almost sharp enough to slice open her skin. "I'm going to have such fun with you. And I'll start by finishing what I started the night before you left. You'd like that, wouldn't you?"

For a moment, she was back in his house, strapped to a table as he carved her hip with a scalpel. Pain lanced through her as her mind sunk deeper and deeper into the memory.

Nell dragged herself back to the present by sheer force of will, the image of Holly and Justin playing in their front yard her only lifeline. "I'm yours, Master, to do with as you please. If you'll please just call Doug, let him know I'm being a good girl—"

His hand moved down to circle her throat, pressing hard enough to send a spike of fear careening down her spine. "I don't think you want to find out what'll happen if you ask me that again."

Panic flooded through her, making her breath come in short, loud gasps. His fingers pressed like bars of steel across her windpipe every time she sucked in more air.

Why wouldn't he make the call? Was it already too late? Were Holly and Justin being hurt even as she knelt here on this fucking path, the packed earth hard as stone beneath her knees?

"What did you do to them? I came! I did what you said. You can't—"

Micah shook her hard enough to make her teeth rattle, and the world spun around her when he finally stopped. "What did I just fucking say? Now get the fuck up." He hauled her up to her feet by her hair, his cruel chuckle ringing in her ears as she bit back a scream. "It's time to take you home where you belong."

That's when a deep voice surged out of the darkness. "You're not taking her anywhere."

"*No!*" She screamed it toward the trees as Micah hauled her back against him, wrapping her up in a bear hug that clamped her arms to her sides. "He hasn't made the call yet!"

"You fucking cunt," Micah growled, his arms constricting so tightly around her chest she could hardly breathe.

"Let her go, O'Neill," Rafe said as he stepped out onto the path. His voice was so low, so deadly calm that it almost didn't feel real. Not when her insides screamed with fear.

"Rafe, please." Tears streamed down her face. "Please go."

His gaze met hers for only a moment, but it was long enough to know he wasn't going anywhere. Keeping up that veneer of absolute calm, he looked past her to Micah. "There's no way for this to end that's good for you. You have to realize that. Let her go and call this whole thing off before it's too late."

"So you're Rafe." Micah didn't seem to have heard Rafe's suggestion. "Even if she didn't tell you she's mine, you must've seen my marks. Only a desperate, weak man would fuck another man's property."

Rafe's smile was hard and cold. "You're the one who can only keep a woman by threatening her."

Oh, for fuck's sake. Antagonizing him would only make things a billion times worse.

Tightening his hold on her, there was a new edge to Micah's voice when he spat out, "I told you not to tell anyone. Guess it's a good thing I already told Doug to have his fun."

"No!" She struggled against his grip as she screamed, her throat aching and raw. "I didn't tell him. Please, I swear I didn't. Do whatever the fuck you want to me. I don't care anymore, just leave them the fuck alone."

"He'll have them by now," Micah said, slamming a forearm into her stomach hard enough that she stopped fighting for several seconds, just trying to breathe. "He's wanted to fuck you for years. Did you know that? But I didn't want him touching what's mine. You wouldn't believe how excited he was when I told him you have a sister who looks just like you. He's probably fucking her right now."

"Actually, he's not." Rafe said it as if he was commenting on the weather. "I just got off the phone with Holly. Turns out her neighbor is a cop."

The truth flew through her like a jet of cool, clear water, putting out the inferno raging inside her in a matter of seconds. "Oh." She sounded almost bored to her own ears. "Well, in that case."

Nell flung her hips to one side so suddenly, Micah didn't have time to react. The force loosened his grip enough that she could throw a fist backward into his groin.

As he doubled over in pain, she ducked and twisted, breaking out of his grip for good, wrenching his arm around in the process. And when

Micah tried to straighten and make a wild grab for her, she slammed the heel of her hand into his nose with the most satisfying *crunch* in the entire fucking world.

He crumpled to the ground like a collapsing house of cards, one hand gripping his crotch, the other trying to stem the gush of blood from his broken nose.

Nell stood over him as he cried and rolled around on the ground, adrenaline singing in her veins. "You," she said, voice ringing out in the night, "will never lay your fucking hands on me again."

CHAPTER 16
Rafe

For the first time in his life, Rafe wanted to kill another human being. But since he was in love with a literal fucking goddess, it seemed that wasn't going to be necessary.

Jonathan and Mason stepped out of the woods behind him, moving up to flank his sides. "While I would certainly understand her desire to do so," Jonathan said, "I suggest you get your girl out of here before she kills him. That'll just make for awkward questions when the police arrive."

Holding up a bundle of rope, Mason added, "We'll take care of the trash."

The three of them moved in together, Rafe heading straight for Nell, the other two circling around to the other side of her still writhing and moaning victim. "Nell?" he said softly, placing a gentle hand on her shoulder.

She jumped at the touch, though she didn't pull away. But she didn't turn to him either, instead glaring down at her ex while her breath came in short gasps, her chest rising and falling so dramatically it looked painful.

Rafe slid his hand toward her neck, until his thumb found her pulse. It was going like a goddamn jackhammer. "Nell," he said again, a little firmer this time. "I think you should come sit down."

It was several seconds before she turned toward him, her gaze slightly unfocused. He had to grab her arm when she tilted precariously to one side. "Everything's spinning," she mumbled, clamping her eyes shut.

"It's all right, sweetheart," he said, scooping her up into his arms. "I've got you." While Jonathan and Mason got to work behind him, he carried her out of the woods, setting her down on the nearest pool chaise.

Zach, Olivia, and Gemma raced across the pool deck as Rafe brushed Nell's hair out of her face. Her skin felt cold and clammy. "When are they getting here?" Rafe demanded, stripping off his wizard's robe and draping it over her. "She needs an ambulance. She's going into shock."

Gemma pushed him out of the way, saying, "I'm a doctor," when he started to object. The sexy little nurse's uniform she wore had certainly been an interesting costume choice.

While she checked Nell's vitals, Zach said, "Aiden's still on the phone with the police. Camden's waiting out front to bring them out here when they arrive. Shouldn't be more than a couple more minutes."

Rafe supposed that was the only downside to living so far away from civilization. Emergency response times weren't exactly top notch.

"Elevate her feet," Gemma instructed. "And someone get her a real blanket. We need to keep her warm."

Zach grabbed a cushion from one of the other chaises while Olivia sprinted toward the house, the feather flying out of her twenties flapper headband and drifting down to the ground.

"Is she going to be okay?" Rafe asked, voice shaking slightly.

Gemma gave him a reassuring smile. "She'll be fine. I don't see anything that worries me. We just need to keep her comfortable until she recovers."

Relief built up in him, leaving his body on a long, heavy sigh. "Thank fuck," he muttered, dropping down onto the chaise across from Gemma. He stroked Nell's hair again and again, letting out another, less dramatic sigh when her breathing started to slow. "That's it. You're all right. Everyone's all right."

He continued to murmur soothing words as the others milled around him—Zach propping up her feet on a cushion, Olivia returning with a huge fluffy blanket and throwing it over her, Gemma repeatedly checking her vitals.

It seemed like an eternity before Aiden and Camden led two police officers out the back door, taking them through the garden at a full run. While Camden led the cops straight to the hiking trail, Aiden slid to a stop at Olivia's side, his twenties gangster fedora askew. "How's she doing?" he asked, wrapping an arm around his fiancée's shoulders.

"She's fine," Gemma answered, smiling. "Aren't you, honey? Do you want to sit up?"

When Nell nodded, Rafe lifted her up, helping her slide backward to lean against the back of the chaise. "You look so much better," he said, cupping her cheek. Thank Christ, her skin felt warm and dry this time.

"You really do," Zach said, perching on the foot of the chaise. "You're getting some of your color back. For a while there, you looked almost gray."

"The paramedics should be here in a minute," Aiden said. "I told them there was a doctor with Nell, so they wanted to check on Sophie first."

Five worried gazes hit him all at once. "What happened to Sophie?" Nell's voice was still weak, but that didn't make it sound any less like a demand.

"Her blood pressure dropped too low after everyone ran out. She fainted. Leo caught her, and she's awake now, but the paramedics aren't taking any chances." Aiden grimaced. "Leo said they just found out last week that she's pregnant again."

When Gemma stiffened, Nell grabbed her arm. "Go. I'm fine, I promise."

With a quick nod, Gemma stood and kicked off her white heels, running toward the mansion barefoot. The whole group watched until the bright white of her skimpy little dress disappeared from sight.

"Thank you," Nell said, her soft, sweet voice breaking the silence. "All of you. I don't know what I would've done without all your help."

Rafe gathered her up against his chest, cradling her there like she was something fragile rather than the total badass she actually was. "You don't have to find out. Not ever again." It was a declaration. A promise. "You're not alone anymore. You don't ever need to go it alone again."

A commotion at the trailhead broke them apart. The whole group turned as one to watch Mason and Jonathan stride from the woods, followed by the two cops. The policemen dragged Micah along between them, the rope bindings replaced by a pair of handcuffs.

Someone had managed to stop Micah's nose from bleeding, though the blood on his face and shirt shone black in the light from the pool. Harsh red lines were visible on his wrists and neck—a souvenir from his time as Mason and Jonathan's captive.

Rafe saw all of that with only a glance. Then his gaze locked on Nell. Now that Micah was taken care of, he didn't have a single fuck left to give about that motherfucker. The only thing that mattered was ensuring Nell was still okay.

Nell watched as the group from the woods drew closer, her gaze never leaving Micah. She didn't even blink. There wasn't a trace of fear in her eyes anymore. Only a cold, burning hatred.

"You fucking whore," Micah said, spitting a glob of blood onto the ground as the cops dragged him past. "Tell them you're mine, or I swear to God, I'll fucking kill you next time I get my hands on you. Tell them you're mine!" He began struggling against the cops, almost managing to wrench his arm out of the shorter one's grip.

Rafe stood, putting his body between Micah and Nell. Zach instantly jumped up beside him, looking scary as hell with his armor and sword, and the others followed suit a moment later, forming a human wall.

The rustling of the blanket and creak of the chaise told him Nell stood behind him. At a gentle tug on his arm, he swung back, letting her step through. Her expression was so cold, it could've been carved from ice. "You try to touch me again, I'll break more than your nose. Now get the fuck out of my sight."

Rafe wanted to jump and throw his fist into the air. Jesus fucking

Christ she was incredible. Instead, he stood like a silent sentinel behind her as the cops got Micah back under control. The taller of the two got them moving toward the house again. "Come on, let's get him out of here. You all, stay at the house. We'll be back to talk to everyone soon."

It occurred to Rafe that a town as small as Fairford maybe only had two or three cops. He never thought about it before. He certainly never saw much of a police presence on his rare trips into town.

Micah must have realized what a big mistake he made, for he didn't speak or struggle again, walking silently between the two officers around the side of the mansion and out of sight.

When Nell's ex was gone at last, Rafe folded his arms around her, kissing the top of her head. "You're the strongest, most amazing woman I've ever met. Do you know that?"

The others gave each other a charged look, and Zach did an exceptionally poor job of hiding his smile. "Why don't we all head inside," Zach said, attempting and failing to achieve a solemn tone. "Let's give these two some privacy."

As Zach herded the others toward the garden gate, Rafe settled down on the chaise, his heart filling near to bursting when she chose to sit on his lap instead of beside him.

"Thank you," Nell said again, resting her cheek against his shoulder. "For coming back. For finding me."

Rafe held her close and sighed. "I'm sorry I left at all." Though he only made it as far as his car after storming out, and hadn't even managed to get in. His heart had been breaking, his mind reeling, but somewhere in the middle of all that, he knew he would regret walking away from her for the rest of his life.

By the time he made it back to Zach's office, Nell was long gone. But an email from Micah was open on the laptop screen. Unable to help himself, he read it.

Thank fucking God he did.

It had taken him about five seconds after that to form a plan. First step: call Holly and warn her. Second step: reinforcements. There wasn't a soul in the Manor who wasn't ready to act in whatever way they could once he explained what was going on.

As soon as Rafe learned about Holly's cop neighbor—who had

already noticed Micah's friend skulking around, arresting him when he tried to break into Holly's house—Aiden had called the Fairford PD. Then it was just a matter of keeping Nell safe until they arrived.

If he hadn't changed his mind—if he hadn't gone back to find her . . .

A shudder tore through him. He couldn't even bear to think about it.

The paramedics came out to find them then, and he welcomed the distraction. He sat by patiently as they checked her vitals, shone light into her eyes, and asked her several questions. When they learned about the blow to her stomach, one of them poked and prodded her belly for over a minute, constantly asking, "Does this hurt?"

In the end, they pronounced her good to go, suggesting she take her over-the-counter pain killer of choice if she had any pain.

They'd been alone again for over a minute before Nell cleared her throat. "I need you to know, I never emailed Micah," Nell said, guilt heavy in her voice. "And I wasn't ever going to. I—"

"I know you weren't," he interrupted. "I'm sorry for how I reacted. It felt like it was happening all over again—you leaving me for someone who could hurt you in ways I wouldn't. Just like Jess. But that wasn't it at all. It's not your fault I panicked."

She sniffed, snuggling into him. "If I hadn't been lying to you, you wouldn't have needed to panic," she pointed out. "I knew you'd be mad I was reading them. I mean, duh. I'm not stupid."

Chuckling, Rafe said, "Indeed."

"But I couldn't stop doing it anyway. Part of me felt *so* good. Getting the apologies, feeling like I was getting some closure on the whole thing. And the other part . . . I think I was waiting for the other shoe to drop. For the act to end and Micah to start emailing me horrible shit again."

"I understand. Of course you wanted it to be real." Rafe began stroking her hair. He'd loved the feel of the long, silky strands between his fingers since the first time he touched them. "But you were too smart to trust it. My good girl."

The tension in her body melted away at his final words. She pulled away, looking up at him through her eyelashes. "Am I your good girl?" she whispered. "It isn't only me, right? You feel the same things I feel?"

Rafe cupped her face between his hands. "If you feel like your heart will wither away and die if we're not together, then yes, I feel exactly the same thing. I—I think I might . . ." He took a deep, bracing breath. "Fuck it. Nell, I love you." Now that he'd finally said it, he wanted to say it a hundred times. A thousand. "Jesus, I love you so fucking much."

Her smile was like a beam of sunlight breaking through the clouds. He wanted to keep this moment with him forever—to memorize every inch of her face. He'd never seen anything more beautiful in his life.

"I love you, too." The tears welling in her eyes caught the blue light from the pool, making her look almost otherworldly. "I love you so much it literally hurts. Can I please touch you? I *need* to touch you right now."

Rafe brushed his lips against hers. "Sweetheart, you don't ever have to ask me that again." Unable to help himself, he smirked. "Unless we're in a scene. Then you'll do as you're told."

Her answering smile heated his blood. "Of course, Sir." Burying her hands in his hair, Nell kissed him as if her life depended on it. He moaned as she fisted her hands, loving the touch of pain.

There was so much shit they needed to figure out. The mess with the police had to be sorted. They had to make sure Sophie and the baby were safe. Nell would surely want to visit her sister as soon as humanly possible. To see that Holly, Justin, and Pete were safe with her own eyes —to continue rebuilding her life.

Then there was the whole matter of whether they'd stay here, move to Tampa, or go somewhere entirely new. Rafe loved the Manor and loved his work, but wherever she went to grad school, that's where Rafe would be.

So much to unravel, so many decisions to be made.

But for now, he lost himself in her taste, in the tiny sounds she made as she claimed him, in the friction of their bodies.

For now, they had each other. And that was all they needed.

EPILOGUE

Nell

Eleven Months Later

"Hold on," Rafe said, pulling her away from the front steps. "I need to carry you over the threshold."

Nell laughed as he scooped her into his arms, carrying her up the three steps to the small, covered front porch. "That's only if you're married, you idiot," she said, smacking his chest.

"You'll quit struggling if you know what's good for you, little girl," he said, though there wasn't a hint of a real threat in his voice. "This is the first house we bought together, and I'm carrying you over the goddamn threshold whether you want me to or not."

Grinning, Nell rested her cheek against his shoulder as he fumbled with the keys, taking it all in. She still couldn't believe this house belonged to them. It seemed like something out of a dream.

They both fell in love with the brick colonial the moment they saw the listing online. The gorgeous old house was exactly what they'd been looking for, with a perfect mix of historic charm and new upgrades that reminded them of the Manor. Just on a much smaller scale.

Even more importantly, it was only a ten-minute walk to the

University of Vermont campus, and not much farther to all the restaurants and shops at Church Street Marketplace in downtown Burlington. Everything they needed was right at their fingertips. And yet, surrounded by trees and tall, sprawling bushes, the house felt isolated and private. With the kinds of games they liked getting up to, they didn't want to feel like judgmental eyes could be on them at any moment.

Somehow, Rafe managed to unlock the front door and push it open without dropping her. "Now you're just being difficult," he complained as she extended her long legs, forcing him to scuttle sideways into the foyer like a crab.

In answer, she wrapped her arms around his neck, pulled herself up, and planted a kiss on his cheek. She giggled as the long strands of his beard tickled her chin. A few months ago, he proudly announced that if he wanted any chance of fitting in with all the hipsters and vegans in Burlington, he needed to grow out his beard.

Nell still wasn't sure if she liked it, but the man was forty years old. If he wanted a long-ass beard, he could have one.

"There," Rafe said, planting her on her feet. "That wasn't so hard, was it?"

Still grinning, she kicked off her flip-flops, wanting to feel the wide, smooth slats of the hardwood beneath her feet. According to the sellers, the floors were original to the house, almost exactly a hundred years old. She fucking loved them.

How many people had stood right here? How many decisions were made, conversations had, lives changed in this exact spot? It was dizzying to think about.

"Movers won't be here for a couple more hours," Rafe said, glancing down at his watch. "We should've brought a couple folding chairs with us. I didn't think about it."

Neither had she. But as she glanced around at the empty living room and dining room, the former to the right of the foyer, the latter to the left, she regretted the oversight. "Hmm," she said, chewing on her bottom lip. "We could maybe walk downtown and get some lunch? We'd be back in plenty of time."

He nodded slowly as he considered the plan. "That sounds like our best bet. But before we go, I want to check something upstairs. Will you come with me?"

Pretending he wasn't being super suspicious, she shrugged and said, "Sure." If he wanted to christen their new bedroom before lunch, she wasn't going to complain. Though she'd insist on being on top. She wasn't getting covered in bruises from the hard-ass floor only days before classes started.

But when they made it to the top of the stairs, he didn't go into the master bedroom. Instead, he led her down the short, narrow hall, stopping at the final door. This was the room she'd claimed as her office, so she had somewhere quiet to do all her schoolwork. The smell of fresh paint was strong even through the closed door.

"What have you been up to?" she asked, narrowing her eyes.

Grinning, he turned the knob, pushing the door open.

Nell gasped, her eyes widening. The room wasn't empty anymore. Most of the floor was covered by a cream and gray patterned rug. An antique desk stood in the corner near the windows, its simple lines matching perfectly with the more modern desk chair. One entire wall was filled by a single bookcase, its shelves reaching almost to the ceiling. And in the center of the room, two cushy armchairs faced one another, a cream-colored ottoman between them.

"It's like my picture," she said, hurrying past him into the room, running her fingers along the top of the desk and sinking a hand into the back of an overstuffed chair. "How did you do this?"

Nell saw her perfect dream office online several months earlier, and fell instantly in love. She'd printed out the picture, determined to have an office just like it someday.

Apparently she didn't have to wait as long as she thought. This room was almost identical, the walls even the same soft, calming blue, the curtains covered in similar embroidery of flowers and vines.

"The desk used to belong to Freya's husband, Ian. She had it shipped up here for you. And I picked out the chairs myself. I wanted to make sure they were the kind you sink into. I know that's what you love." With a proud smile, he finished with, "Aiden and I made the bookcase."

"You made this?" She couldn't keep the disbelief out of her voice. It looked like something out of an expensive-ass furniture store, the wood stained gray and partially painted for a gorgeous industrial look.

He beamed at her. "These hands can do more than spank, you know."

Laughing, she spun around, still trying to take it all in. "I can't believe this. I swear this is the same exact rug."

"You'll have to thank Zach for that," he admitted. "He made it his personal mission to get this room as close to your picture as possible."

Nell dropped down into one of the armchairs, grinning. "So *that's* what he's been doing. I knew he was up to something."

Ever since Nell and Rafe had announced their plans to the rest of the Manor partners and staff, Zach spent long stretches of time holed away in his office, scrolling through pages on his laptop nonstop and spending far more time on the phone than his job usually required. She couldn't wait to see him, so she could give him a giant hug.

"You know how he is," Rafe said, settling down in the second chair. "Once he gets an idea into his head, he doesn't rest until he makes it happen. The man is unstoppable."

That was true enough. As soon as Nell told him her plan to earn a master's degree, he spent countless hours researching therapist licensing requirements in various states, plus programs at grad schools all over the country. When a printout about the graduate counseling program at the University of Vermont appeared on her bedside table one day, she had no trouble figuring out who put it there.

UVM was only an hour and a half from the Manor and had a fantastic program. Not the best commute in the world, but Rafe was more than willing if that's what it took for both of them to have their dream jobs. She didn't even mind that he'd have to stay in Fairford overnight now and again. The idea that Rafe could keep working at the Manor while she got her degree was too good to pass up.

"All right, let's go get lunch," Rafe said, struggling out of the marshmallow-like chair. He grabbed her hands and hauled her to her feet. "Zach came down for the day to supervise the work on your office, and he's waiting for us at that farm-to-table restaurant you keep talking about."

This day just kept getting better and better. Nell practically skipped back through the house, sliding her flip-flops on before heading out the front door.

"So," Rafe said as they strolled down the front path to the sidewalk. "Only two more days until you're officially a grad student. I kind of think that deserves a reward."

Nell laughed. "The dream office isn't my reward?"

Waving a dismissive hand, Rafe said, "That was a gift. A gift is very different from a reward."

"If you say so," she said, rolling her eyes. "So what do you have in mind?"

"Oh, I don't know." He gave her a sly look out of the corner of his eye. "Maybe another fantasy?"

Nell's brows shot upward. "Now that," she said, tapping a finger against her chin, "is a very enticing proposition."

"Anything on your list we haven't tried yet?" Rafe asked, grinning down at her. "Maybe that one you didn't want to tell me last year? If you're ready to, I mean."

Her lips spread into a slow smile. A very enticing proposition indeed.

She hadn't known Rafe well enough last October. For this fantasy to work, she needed to trust her partner implicitly. Not only trust he'd keep her mind and body safe, but also that he understood the part of her that wanted this.

Going up onto her toes, Nell whispered into his ear. By the time she settled back on her heels, Rafe's gray-green eyes glittered with excitement. "That can be arranged."

Nell was fucking *exhausted*. Her first week of grad school had been simultaneously incredible and terrifying. She adored the classes, but damn it was a fuck ton of work. Only a week in, and already she stayed up late working every night. She didn't even want to think about all the unpacking they still had to do.

Part of her was terrified she wouldn't be able to keep up. The fact that she was more than a decade older than all the other students didn't help. If it wasn't for Rafe's daily reassurances (and frequent shoulder and foot rubs), she might have given into her fears by now.

Switching the strap of her messenger bag to her other shoulder, she hurried her steps, eager to be home. She had a metric ton of homework and reading to do this weekend, but it could wait until Sunday. Rafe promised to be waiting for her when she got there, and she wanted to spend the next thirty-six hours in that man's arms.

Or with her mouth around his cock. Whichever.

That delectable image only made her feet move faster. She was practically jogging by the time she hurried up the front walk and onto the porch. If Rafe wasn't inside one of her holes within the next five minutes—she didn't care which one—she might just scream.

"Rafe?" She looked around for him as soon as she pushed the door open, disappointed when she didn't find him on the living room sofa. "Where are you?"

There was no answer.

Frowning, she shut the door behind her, turning the deadbolt. He'd planned to spend the whole day unpacking, wanting the house to be ready when Holly, Pete, Justin, and her mom flew out next week. Though he tried to hide it, he was definitely nervous about making the right impression—especially on her mom. She could tell he was afraid of ruining the rocky relationship they'd managed to build in the last year.

After all that work, maybe he was up in the shower? As sexy as it was to imagine licking salty sweat off his skin, she had to admit a clean Rafe sounded far more appealing than a filthy one.

Leaving her bag and sandals by the front door, she made her way upstairs. "Rafe?" she called out again, crossing the hall to the closed master bedroom door. Light peeked out from the gap at the bottom, but she couldn't hear the shower running. Was he even home? Opening the door, she stepped inside, gaze sweeping the room for any sign of him.

That's when someone grabbed her from behind. Strong arms encircled her, crushing her arms against her sides with enough force that she cried out.

Micah. He swore he'd kill her.

But no, she knew for a fact his ass was still in jail. And the arms around her were far too large, way too strong.

Her self-defense training kicked in. Nell threw her hips to one side, wanting to throw him off balance and loosen his arms. This man seemed to anticipate the move, though, and shifted with her, his arms like a python crushing her ribs.

When she tried to slam her heel down on her captor's foot, he dodged with ease, then lifted her off the ground entirely. "Rafe!" She screamed it at the top of her lungs, hoping he was off in some other corner of the house and just hadn't heard her get home.

If this person had attacked him, if Rafe was hurt somewhere . . .

She screamed his name again, twisting and writhing, kicking and flailing, doing every damn thing in her power to break the man's grip. All the agitation made his right sleeve ride up his arm, revealing part of a tattoo.

It was a monochrome eagle, wings outspread.

Rafe.

And then she remembered. Her fantasy.

For the space of three seconds, she went completely still. That was enough for him to throw her facedown on the bed, pinning her down with his hands and knees.

Oh, it was fucking *on*.

Nell redoubled her efforts, throwing her weight from side to side, trying to throw him off. But he was too heavy. Too strong.

Keeping her legs pinned to the mattress with his knees, he wrenched her arms behind her back, wrapping one enormous hand around her wrists.

"Get the fuck off me!" Nell shouted, bucking her hips, trying to pull her hands free. "I swear to fucking God, when my boyfriend gets home, he's going to fucking kill you. Now get off me before I—" A scream tore out of her, cutting the threat short.

He'd twisted her arms up behind her so far, it felt like something was about to tear.

"Enough." His voice was like smoke and gravel. It sent a chill of terror running down the length of her spine. "Be still or I'll dislocate both your shoulders."

The warning distracted her just long enough. By the time she started fighting again, he already had a rope looped around both her wrists. It was easy enough for him to control her as he tied it off, manipulating the ends into a complicated knot.

He let go of her arms then, sitting back as she wore herself out trying to stretch the rope. But no matter how she pulled and twisted, it had no give.

She was so fucked.

When at last Nell's muscles went limp, her upper body sinking into the mattress, he stood.

The second her legs were free, she kicked back, aiming for what she hoped was his groin. He must've expected the attack, because she hit nothing but air.

"You're making this harder on yourself," he scolded, grabbing her around the ankle with both hands, jerking her leg up until her quads fucking burned with the strain. She kicked out feebly with the other leg, but it was a pathetic effort. He got a rope knotted around her ankle in seconds flat, then slammed her leg down to the bed so he could tie the other end of the rope to the corner post.

Nell tried to roll. To get onto her back and kick upward with her free leg before he could tie that one down too. Anything to stop herself from being completely immobilized.

But it was as if he could read her fucking mind. No matter what she did, no matter how she moved, he seemed to know exactly how to counter it.

He pushed her deeper into the mattress, keeping her stuck on her belly. With both hands and one leg already neutralized, it was humiliating how easily he tied her left leg to the other post.

"There," he said, running his hands up the insides of her spread thighs. "Much better."

Her eyes fluttered closed as he moved his hands up over her shorts, cupping her ass through the denim. She clenched her lips together as he squeezed, biting back a moan.

"That's it," he said, kneading her ass, pushing her hips down onto the bed every time she lifted them into his hands. "You want this, don't you, you little slut? You want me to fuck you. You want me to force you."

She opened her mouth to object, and the moan she'd been swallowing came tumbling out instead. Pressing her face into the comforter, she tried to muffle the sound, but it was too late. He already heard it.

"What a dirty little slut you are," he said, landing a volley of hard spanks across the center of her ass. Even through the thick denim, they stung like hell. "Now be still. It's time to get these clothes off you, and I don't want to cut you."

Nell froze when the cold metal tip of scissors touched her upper thigh. "Please." It came out like a whimper. "Please don't do this. You don't have to do this."

His laugh sent goosebumps erupting across her skin. "But we've already established you want me to." The metallic *snip* of the scissors hit her like gunfire in the silent room, battering against her ears again and again, consuming all her thoughts.

He cut her clothes away piece by piece, until there was nothing left to protect her body from him. "Mmm," he said, sliding a finger easily into her pussy, pumping it in and out of her. "I knew you were a slut the first time I saw you. Look how wet you are for me. How much your body wants me."

"No," she said, even as her pussy clenched around him, trying to draw his finger deeper. "I'll never want you."

Grabbing a fistful of her hair, he yanked her head a few inches above the bed. "Naughty little girls who can't stop lying get punished. Open your mouth." When she didn't immediately obey, he slapped her face—not hard enough to leave a mark, but enough to startle her into obedience.

The moment her lips parted, he stuffed a ball of black fabric into her mouth. "Taste it," he growled, pressing it against her tongue. "Taste what a liar you are."

Holy fuck, he gagged her with her own panties.

Clit throbbing and pussy spasming, all she could do was wait. Wait for him to take her and prove beyond a shadow of a doubt what a fucking liar she was.

Leaving the panties in her mouth, he lifted her hips, shoving a pillow underneath. Then he moved to the foot of the bed, kneeling on the mattress between her spread legs, his hands on either side of her head. Before she knew what was happening, he entered her, bottoming out on the first stroke.

Nell tried to scream. To beg for more. To moan like the fucking whore she was as he pulled out and slammed back in, the ropes on her ankles so tight she couldn't even rock forward. But satin and lace still filled her mouth, some of the fabric spilling out between her lips. All she could do was lie there, ass in the air, cheek pressed against the comforter, as he pounded into her again and again.

When he switched up his angle so he hit her G-spot on every thrust, holy motherfucking shit, she literally felt like she could die. Right here. Right now.

Her orgasm hit her so fast and hard, she thought she might be having a fucking stroke. She screamed when he ripped the panties from her mouth, her pussy clenching around him so hard his moan was more pain than pleasure.

Nell actually cried when he pulled out, rocking her hips back, incoherent words tumbling out of her mouth. Hell, it could've been gibberish. All she knew was that if he wasn't back inside her in the next thirty seconds, she was going to die.

"We don't need these anymore, do we little slut?" Glee filled his smoke and gravel voice as he picked apart the knot at her wrists and tossed the rope onto the floor. With two snips of his scissors, her legs were also free.

She didn't fight him as he ripped the pillow out from under her and flipped her onto her back. The thought never even crossed her mind.

"That's my good little slut," he said, pushing her legs wider apart, sliding her down to the end of the bed.

Nell wrapped her legs around his hips, digging her heels into his ass to draw him closer. "Please, please, please, please—" Her mouth fell open on a gasp as he slid into her.

"That's it," Rafe said, lifting her hips slightly, pulling her toward him each time his hips surged forward. "Show me how much you love this. Touch yourself. Make yourself come again."

Her finger was on her clit before he even finished speaking. Holy shit, it was so good, so fucking good. "I love you," she gasped out, screwing her eyes shut as her finger moved faster and faster, and he pounded into her so hard the headboard might break through the fucking wall. "Oh my God, I love you, I love you, I lo—" The word never made it out, swallowed up by her scream as she came again.

Rafe's harsh shout joined hers, his last several thrusts jerky and erratic as he came deep inside of her. "Jesus fucking Christ," he murmured, pulling out and flopping down onto the bed beside her. "Nell, that was—it was—*fuck*." He struggled to catch his breath. Rolling over onto his side, he traced a fingertip down her arm. "I love you, too. God, I love you so fucking much."

It took an eternity for Nell to regain her senses. Every nerve ending in her body tingled in the most glorious way. And Rafe kept that delicious, shivery sensation going, tracing a pattern on her right hip over and over—the outline of butterfly wings.

Mere days after Micah's arrest, Rafe showed her an intricate drawing of a butterfly, wings spread wide. It looked exactly like the one they saw out in the garden—the same white and yellow-orange spots on shimmering black wings. Those iridescent blue patches near the bottom. The spotted body and long antennae that curled at the end.

He had his longtime tattoo artist draw it for her as a surprise. "Zero pressure at all," he assured her, sounding almost nervous. "It's your body, and you can put whatever ink on it you damn well please. But I know you wanted another butterfly on your hip and, well . . . I just thought it might be good to cover up such a terrible memory with a better one."

Nell had flung herself into his arms, kissing every single inch of him she could reach. They drove down to Massachusetts to have the tattoo done a few weeks later.

Rolling her head to the side, she opened her eyes at last, watching as Rafe traced the butterfly's wings, a soft, gentle smile playing at the corners of his lips.

"Thank you," she said, running her fingers through his hair, loving the way he leaned into her touch. "That was so much better than I imagined. You somehow manage to make all my dreams a million times more than I ever thought they could be."

Capturing her hand in his, Rafe pulled it down, pressing his lips against the inside of her wrist. "I should be the one thanking you. I forgot how to dream before you came into my life and reminded me."

Tears welled in her eyes as she smiled. "I won't let you forget again. I promise."

The End

Acknowledgments

First and foremost, I couldn't have possibly done this without Linda Russell and the rest of the team at Foreword PR & Marketing. I'll be forever grateful for your expertise and kindness.

A huge, never-ending thank you to my incredible editor, Karen Washo at Utterly Unashamed. I forgive you for hating exclamation points—mostly because you were right every single time. Thank you for whipping this book into shape, and for yet another phenomenal blurb. You truly have a gift.

Every book is inevitably judged by its cover, which is why Robin Johnson at Florida Girl Design is the absolute best. The first time I saw the paperback cover with the butterfly, I cried. Thank you for creating the most beautiful covers in the world for me. And a very special thank you to Cadwallader Photography, LLC for the stunning photo used in the eBook cover. As soon as I saw this picture, I knew they were meant to be Rafe and Nell.

I can't thank Shari Ryan at MadHat Studios enough for my beautiful interior formatting. Same goes for Virginia Carey, my brilliant proof-reader. When I started this whole endeavor, my goal was for my book to be indistinguishable from something put out by a major publishing house. Thanks to you two, I think I've succeeded.

And of course, thank you to my husband Jason. None of this would be possible without your love and support. You're the most wonderful human I've ever had the privilege of knowing, and I love you as big as the whole universe.

About the Author

Bay Sinclair is the author of steamy romance with broken girls, sexy Doms, and lots of heart. She writes contemporary romance—though she was one credit away from a history minor in college, and historical romances hold a special place in her heart. When she isn't writing, she's an avid foodie in search of the next great culinary adventure, and she drinks entirely too much green tea.

Connect Online
BaySinclair.com

facebook.com/100092035117400

x.com/authorbsinclair

instagram.com/authorbsinclair